D0252998

. . .

IN HIS LONG AND RICH CAREER, Arthur Miller has charted some of the most hidden aspects of the American character, and made us recognize ourselves. With *Homely Girl, A Life*, he turns his attention to a smaller, more intimate canvas, but one that in its deceptive delicacy still encompasses a vast range of human fears, ambitions, desires. It is an exquisite portrait of a woman finding a language to describe herself—a fierce search that pits her against the smothering expectations of her husband and her age.

Flanked by two other stories also set in pre- and post-war Manhattan, this collection pays homage to a city constantly reinventing itself, and to the powerful Miller themes of identity, culpability, and honor. Viking is pleased to mark the occasion of Arthur Miller's eightieth birthday with these masterful stories that show all the precision and greatness of spirit of his classic plays.

ARTHUR MILLER was born in New York City in 1915 and studied at the University of Michigan. He is the author of sixteen plays, including *All My Sons, Death of a Salesman, The Crucible, A View From the Bridge, Incident at Vichy, The Price*, and, most recently, *Broken Glass*, which won the 1995 Olivier Award for best play. He has also written two novels, several collections of reportage, and a memoir, *Timebends*. He has twice won the New York Drama Critics Circle Award, and in 1949 he was awarded the Pulitzer Prize.

HOMELY GIRL, A LIFE

and other stories

ALSO BY ARTHUR MILLER

Arthur Miller by Alexander Calder, 1971

ARTHUR MILLER

HOMELY GIRL, A LIFE

and other stories

VIKING

VIKING
Published by the Penguin Group
Penguin Books USA Inc., 375 Hudson Street,
New York, New York 10014, U.S.A.
Penguin Books Ltd, 27 Wrights Lane, London W8 5TZ, England
Penguin Books Australia Ltd, Ringwood, Victoria, Australia
Penguin Books Canada Ltd, 10 Alcorn Avenue,
Toronto, Ontario, Canada M4V 3B2
Penguin Books (N.Z.) Ltd, 182–190 Wairau Road,
Auckland 10, New Zealand

Penguin Books Ltd, Registered Offices:
Harmondsworth, Middlesex, England

First published in 1995 by Viking Penguin,
a division of Penguin Books USA Inc.

1   3   5   7   9   10   8   6   4   2

"Homely Girl, A Life" was first published as an edition with illustrations by
Louise Bourgeois by Peter Blum Books, 1992. "Fame" first appeared as "The
Recognitions" in *Esquire*, July 1966. "Fitter's Night" originally appeared in Mr.
Miller's *I Don't Need You Anymore*, Viking, 1967.

LIBRARY OF CONGRESS CATALOGING IN PUBLICATION DATA
Miller, Arthur, 1915–
Homely girl, a life, and other stories/Arthur Miller.
p.   cm.
ISBN 0–670–86541–9 (alk. paper)
1. United States—Social life and customs—20th century—Fiction.
I. Title.
PS3525.I5156H67   1995
813'.52—dc20   95–14267

This book is printed on acid-free paper
∞

Printed in the United States of America
Set in Janson
Designed by Francesca Belanger

2.23.2006 Berkeley, CA

CONTENTS

HOMELY GIRL, A LIFE

I

A COLD WIND seemed to blow on her as she surfaced from a deep sleep. Yesterday had been warm in Central Park, and it was June. Opening her eyes as usual toward him, she saw how strangely blanched his face was. Although what she called his sleeping smile was still there, and the usual suggestion of happiness at the curled corners of his mouth, he seemed heavier on the mattress. And she knew immediately and with dread raised her hand and touched his cheek—the end of the long story. Her first thought, like an appeal against a mistake: But he is only sixty-eight!

Fright but no tears, not outside. Just the thump on the back of her neck. Life had a fist.

"Ah!" she pitied aloud, and bringing palms together, she touched fingers to her lips. "Ah!" She bent to him, her silky hair touching his face. But he wasn't there. "Ah, Charles!" A little anger soon dispersed by reason. And wonder.

The wonder remained—that after all her life had amounted to a little something, had given her this man, this man who had never seen her. He was awesome now, lying there.

Oh, if one more time she could have spoken with him, asked or told him . . . what? The thing in her heart, the wonder. That he had loved her and had never seen her in the fourteen years of their life. There was always, despite everything, something in her trying to move itself into his line of vision, as though with one split-second glimpse of her his fluttering eyes would wake from their eternal sleep.

Now what do I do? Oh, Charles dear, what do I do with the rest of it?

Something was not finished. But I suppose, she said to herself, nothing ever is except in movies when the lights come on, leaving you squinting on the sidewalk.

Once more, she moved to touch him, but already he was not there, not hers, not anything, and she withdrew her hand and sat there with one leg hanging over the mattress.

She hated her face as a girl but knew she had style and at least once a day settled for that and her very good compact body and a terrific long neck. And yes, her irony. She was and wanted to be a snob. She knew how to slip a slight, witty rotation into her hips when she walked, although she had no illusions it made up for a pulled look to her cheeks, as if alum had tightened her skin, and an elongated upper lip. A little like Disraeli, she thought once, coming on his picture in a high-school text. And a too-high forehead (she refused to overlook anything negative). She wondered if she'd been drawn out of the womb and lengthened, or her mother startled by a giraffe. At parties she had many a time noticed how men coming up behind her were caught surprised when she turned to face them. But she had learned to shake out the straight silky light-brown hair and flick the ironic defensive grin, silent pardon for their inevitable fade. She had a tonic charm and it was almost enough, although not quite, of course, not since childhood when her mother held up a *Cosmopolitan* Ivory ad to her face and so warmly and lovingly exclaimed, "Now that's beauty!" as though by staring at it hard enough she could be made to look like one of those girls. She felt blamed then. Still, at fifteen she believed that between her ankles and her breasts she was as luscious as Betty Grable, or almost. And she had a soft, provocative lisp that men who had an interest in mouths seemed to like. At sixteen, she'd been told by Aunt Ida, visiting from Egypt, "You've got an Egyptian look; Egyptian women are hot." Recalling that oddity would make her laugh and would raise her spirits even into her sixties, after Charles had died.

A number of memories involved lying in bed on a Sunday morning, listening thankfully to muffled New York outside. "I was just thinking, apropos of nothing," she whispered into Charles's ear one time, "that for at least a year after Sam and I had separated, I was terribly embarrassed to say we had. And even after you and I married, whenever I had to refer to 'my first husband' it curdled something inside me. Like a disgrace or a defeat. What a simpleminded generation we were!"

Sam was beneath her in some indefinite class sense, but that was part of his attraction to the thirties, when to have been born to money was shameful, a guarantee of futility. People her age, early twenties then, wanted to signify by doing good, attended emergency meetings a couple of times a week in downtown lofts or sympathizers' West End Avenue living rooms to raise money for the new National Maritime Union or buying ambulances for the Spanish Republicans, and they were moved to genuine outrage by Fascism, which was somehow a parents' system and the rape of the mind; the Socialist hope was for the young, for her, and no parent could help but fear its subversive beauty. So political talk was mostly avoided at home. Anyway, hers were hopelessly silly people, Jews putting on the dog with a new, absurd name endowed by the Immigration inspectors back in the other century because Great-grandpa's original Russian one was unpronounceable by their Irish tongues. So they were Sessions.

But Sam was Fink, which she rather relished as a taunt to her father, long a widower and very ill now but still being consulted on the phone as an authority on utilities by the time of her marriage, dying as he read that Hitler had walked into Vienna. "But he won't last," he whispered scoffingly across the cancer in his throat. "The Germans are too intelligent for this idiot." But of course by now she knew better, knew a world was ending, and would not be surprised to see American storm troopers with chin straps on Broadway one evening. It was already scary to go walking around in Yorkville on the Upper East Side, where the Germans were rallying on the street corners to bait Jews and praise Hitler on summertime Saturday nights. She was not particularly Semitic-looking, but she feared the fear of the prey as she passed thick-necked men on Eighty-sixth Street.

In her teens, she wondered: I am never going to be beautiful or even a genius. What am I supposed to expect then? She felt surrounded by too much space and longed for a wall to have to climb over.

A stylish man, her father, with a long, noble head and an outmoded mind, or so she thought of him in the flush of her newfound revolutionary independence. Stroking his cold hand in the gloom of the West End Avenue apartment, she thanked her luck, or rather her own perceptive intelligence, which had helped turn her away from all this heavy European silverware, the overstuffed chairs and the immense expanse of Oriental carpet, the sheer doomed weight of their tea service and the laughable confidence it had once expressed. If not beautiful, she was at least strong, free of Papa's powerful illusions. But now that he was weak and his eyes closed most of the time, she could let herself admit that she shared his arrogant style, caring a lot and pretending not to, unlike her mother, who'd screamingly pretended to care and hadn't cared at all. But of course Papa accepted the injustice in the world as natural as trees. Outwardly a conventional man, he was quickly bored by predictable people, and this had conspiratorially linked her to him. She delighted in his covert mockery of uniformity, which fueled her rebellion against her mother. A day before he died, he smiled at her and said, "Don't worry, Janice, you're pretty enough, you'll be okay, you've got the guts." If only okay could ever be enough.

The rabbi's brief ceremony must have been developed for these bankrupt times; people were scanting even rote funerary farewells to get back to their gnawing make-a-living worries. Following the prayer, the funeral chapel man, looking like H. L. Mencken, with hair parted in the middle, shot his starched cuffs and picked up the small cardboard box of ashes, handing it to her fat brother, Herman, who in his surprise looked at it as if it were a ticking explosive. Then they went out into the hot sunlit street and walked downtown together. Herman's butterball wife, Edna, kept falling behind to look into an occasional shoe store window, one of the few shops still occupied in whole blocks of vacancies along Broadway. Half of New York seemed to be for rent, with permanent "Vacancy" signs bolted to nearly every apartment house entrance. Now, eight years after the Crash, the heads of the bolts were beginning to rust. Herman walked flopping his feet down like a seal and sucked for breath. "Look at it, the whole block," he said with a wave of his hand.

"Real estate doesn't interest me right now," Janice said.

"Oh, it doesn't? Maybe eating does, 'cause this is where Papa put a lot of your money, baby." They entered a darkened Irish bar on Eighty-fourth Street facing Broadway and sat with an electric fan blowing into their faces. "Did you hear? Roosevelt's supposed to have syph."

"I'm trying to drink this, please." Defying ritual and capitalist superstition, she wore a beige skirt and a shiny white silk blouse and high-heeled tan shoes. Sam had to be in Syracuse to bid on an important library being auctioned. "You must be the last Republican Jew in New York," she said.

Herman wheezed, absently moving the little box around on the bar like the final beleaguered piece in a lost chess game, a futile three inches in one direction and then in the other. He sipped his beer and talked about Hitler, the remorseless heat that summer, and real estate.

"These refugees are coming over and buying up Amsterdam Avenue."

"So what difference does that make?"

"Well, they're supposed to be so downtrodden."

"You want them more downtrodden? Don't you understand anything? Now that Franco's won, Hitler's going to attack Russia, there's going to be a tremendous war. And all you can think of is real estate."

"So what if he attacks Russia?"

"Oh God, I'm going home." Disgust flowed up her back, and glancing at the little box, she drank her second martini fast; how really weird, a whole man fitting into a four-by-six-inch carton hardly big enough for a few muffins.

"If you'd throw some of your share in with mine, we could pick up buildings for next to nothing. This Depression won't last forever, and we could clean up someday."

"You really know how to pick a time to talk about business."

"Did you read? No rain in Oklahoma; it's starting to blow away again."

He had all Papa's greed but none of his charm, with a baby face and pudgy hands. Slipping off her stool, smiling angrily, she gave him a monitory bop on the head with her purse, kissed Edna's plump cheek, and with heels clacking walked into the street, Herman behind her defending his right to be interested in real estate.

She was halfway home in the taxi when she recalled that at some point he had bequeathed the ashes to her. Had he remembered to take them from the bar? She called him. Scandalized, he piped, "You mean you lost them?" She hung up, cutting him off, scared. She had left Papa on the bar. She went weak in the thighs with some superstitious fear that she had to force out of her mind. After all, she thought, what is the body? Only the *idea* of a person matters, and Papa's in my heart. Running a bath and flowing toward transcendence again in the remnants of her yellow martini haze, she glimpsed her unchangeable face in the steamy mirror and the body mattered again. Yet at the same time it didn't. She tried to recall a classical philosopher who might have reconciled the two truths, but tired of the effort. Then, realizing she had bathed only a few hours earlier, she shut off the tap and began to dress again.

She found she was hurrying and knew she had to get the ashes back; she had done an awful thing, leaving them there, something like sin. For a moment her father lived, reprimanding her with a sad look. But why, despite everything, was there something funny in the whole business? How tasteless she was!

The bartender, a thin, long-armed man, recalled no such box. He asked if there was anything valuable in it, and she said, "Well, no." Then the guilt butted her like a goat. "My father. His ashes."

"Holy Jesus!" The man's eyes widened at this omen of bad luck. His flaring emotion startled her into weeping. It was the first time, and she felt grateful to him and also ashamed that he might feel more about Papa than she did. He touched her back with his hand and guided her to the dismal ladies' room in the rear, but looking around, she found nothing. The man was odorless, like Vaseline, and for a split instant she wondered if this was all a dream. She stared down at the toilet. Oh God, what if someone sprinkled Papa down there! Returning to the bar, she touched the man's thick tattooed forearm. "It doesn't matter," she reassured him. He insisted on giving her a drink and she had a martini, and they talked about different kinds of death, sudden and drawn out, the deaths of the very young and the old. Her eyes were red-rimmed. Two gas company workers at the bar listened in their brutal solemnity from a respectful distance. It had always been more relaxing for her to be among strange men than with women she didn't know. The bartender came around the bar to see her to the door, and before she could think, she kissed him on the cheek. "Thank you," she said. Sam had never really pursued her, she thought now; she had more or less granted herself to him. She walked down Broadway, angering at their marriage, and by the time she reached the corner loved, or at least pitied, him again.

And so Papa was gone. After a few blocks she felt relieved as she sensed the gift of mourning in her, that illusion of connection with a past; but how strange that the emotion should have been given her by a probably right-wing Catholic Irishman who no doubt was a supporter of Franco and couldn't stand Jews. Everything was feeling, nothing was clear. But she rejected that idea at once. "If feeling is everything, I might as well settle for being my mother." Too awful. Somehow, in this sudden, unexpected collision with the barman's direct feeling, she saw that she really must stop waiting to become someone else: she was Janice forever. What an exciting idea if she could only follow it; maybe it would lead her to solid ground. This endless waiting-to-become was like the Depression itself—everybody kept waiting for it to lift and forgot how to live in the meantime, but supposing it went on forever? She must start living! And Sam had to start thinking of something else than Fascism and organizing unions and the rest of the endlessly repetitious radical agenda. But she mustn't think that way, she guiltily corrected herself.

She smiled, perversely reminded of her new liberation. No parents! I am an orphan. In a few minutes, walking down Broadway, she saw something amusing in so formal and fastidious a man as Dave Sessions being left in a box on a bar: she could see him trapped in there, tiny, outraged, and red-faced, banging on the lid to be let out. A strange thought struck her—that the body was more of an abstraction than the soul, which never disappeared.

Sam Fink had a warming smile, an arched bony nose, which, as he said, he had been years learning to love. He was just about Janice's five feet seven, and standing face-to-face with him sometimes brought to mind her mother's nastily repeated warning, "Never marry a handsome man," a barely disguised jab not only at beautiful Papa's vanity but at her daughter's looks. But unhandsome Sam, absolutely devoted to her, had a different beauty, the excitement of the possessed. His Communist commitment turned her to the future and away from what she regarded as her nemesis, triviality, the bourgeois obsession with things.

Nevertheless, it was painful to look at pictures in museums with him at her side—she had majored in art history at Hunter—and to hear nothing about Picasso but his conversion to the Party, or about the secret antimonarchical codes buried in Titian's painting or the class-struggle metaphor in Rembrandt. "They are not necessarily conscious of it, of course, but the great ones were always in a struggle with the ruling class."

"But, darling, all that has nothing to do with painting."

And, spoken with a teacher's gently superior grin toward a child—and incipient violence buried deep in his eyes: "Except that it has everything to do with painting; their convictions were what raised them above the others, the 'painters.' You have to learn this, Janice: conviction matters."

She felt love in his voice, and so she was somehow reassured by what she did not quite believe. Tucking her arm under his as they walked, she supposed most people married not out of overwhelming love but to find justification in one another, and why not? Glancing at his powerful nose and neat, nearly bald head, she felt elevated by his moral nature and safe in his militancy. But it was not always possible to banish the vision of an empty space surrounding them, a lightless gloom out of which something horrible could suddenly pounce one day. Unconsciously, she began waiting for its appearance, a rending explosion from below.

It was his amazing knowledge of books that helped quiet her doubts. Sam, unusual among book dealers, read or at least skimmed what he was selling, and could pick out of the air the names of authorities on a couple of hundred of subjects from Chess to China, as he snappily put it to his awed customers, who forgave his arrogance for the research it saved them from having to do. He knew the locations of dozens of old mansions all over New York State, Connecticut, Massachusetts, and New Jersey where expiring old families still had sizable libraries to get rid of on the death of some final aunt, uncle, or inheriting retainer. A couple of times a month, he would drive into the country in his green stiff-sprung Nash for a day or two and return with trunk and back seat packed with sets of Twain, Fenimore Cooper, Emerson, Dickens, Poe, Thackeray, Melville, Hawthorne, and Shakespeare, and armfuls of arcane, mouse-nibbled miscellany—*John Keats' Secret*, an 1868 *Survey of Literature of the Womb*, a 1905 *Manual of Chinese Enamelware*, *Lasting Irish Melodies* of 1884, *Annals of Ophthalmology*, or *A Speculation on Ancient Egyptian Surgery*. Janice would sit with Sam on the floor of their dark East Thirty-second Street living room, she imagining the silent, sealed-up life of the family in some upper Monroe County household from whose privacy these books had been ripped, books that must once have brought news of the great world out and beyond their lilac doorways.

Watching him thumb through his finds, she thought he had the ethereal look of a cute monk, including the innocent round tonsure. Was it his sheer goodness that annoyed her? There was something monkish in his pretense of not noticing—when she leaned back resting on her elbows, one leg tucked under and her skirt midway up her thigh—that she was asking to be taken there on the floor. When she saw him flush and shift to some explication of the day's news, a fury flashed and died away within her, and she despaired for herself. Still, with Britain and France secretly flirting with Fascism, she could hardly ask him to set her greedy desire ahead of serious things.

But his plain love for his books and his work stirred her love for him. With the proprietary self-congratulation of an author, he would read choice passages to her, from Trollope especially, or Henry James or Virginia Woolf, or Communist Louis Aragon and the young Richard Wright. He was snobbish like her but, unlike her, denied it.

Alone at least two evenings a week, when Sam went to Party meetings, she walked across the dead East Side over to slummy Sixth with its tenements and dusty Irish bars under the el and came home tired to listen to Benny Goodman records and smoke too many Chesterfields until she was tensed and angry at the walls. When Sam came home explicating Stalin's latest utterances on how the Socialist future, bearing goodness at last, was moving as inexorably toward them as an ocean wave, she nearly drowned in her own ingratitude and was only restored for the moment by the vision of justice that he was guarding, along with the nameless army of civilized comrades spread out across every country in the world.

On another Sunday morning in bed with Charles, forever trying to visualize herself, she said, "I can never figure out what got me; it was about four years after being married;

we'd usually come home from a French or Russian movie on Irving Place and go to bed, and that was that. This time I decided to make myself a martini and then sat on the couch listening to records, you know, like Benny Goodman's 'A Train' or the Billie Holiday things or Ledbetter, or maybe Woody Guthrie, I think, was coming on at that time, and after twenty minutes Sam came out of the bedroom in his pajamas. He was really shy but he wasn't a coward, and he stood there, poor man, with that tense grin, leaning on the bedroom doorjamb like Humphrey Bogart, and he said, 'Sleeptime.' "

"That's when it just fell out of my mouth. 'Fuck the future,' I said."

Charles's eyes fluttered and he laughed with her and pressed his hand on the inside of her thigh.

"He laughed, but blushing—you know, that I'd said that word. And he said, 'What does that mean?' "

"Just fuck the future." She heard her own tinkling giggle and would always remember the free-falling feeling in her chest.

"It must have a meaning."

"It means that there must be something happening now that is interesting and worth thinking about. And now means now."

"Now always means now." He grinned against apprehension.

"No, it mostly means pretty soon, or someday. But now it means tonight."

Angered, he blushed deeper, right up his high forehead, into his hair. She opened the dark oak cabinet and made another martini and giggling at some secret joke got into bed and drank it to the bottom. Feeling left out, he could only go on idealistically grinning, brave man, elbow on the pillow, trying hard to get a grasp on her spinning mind.

"Papa and I once lived in this Portuguese beach house for a month after Mama died, and I used to watch this peasant cook we had when she'd come over the sand dunes carrying fresh vegetables and a fish in a basket for me to inspect so she could cook it for us. She'd take forever trudging in the sand till she got to me, and then all it was was this fish, which was still damp from the ocean."

"What about it?"

"Well, that's it—you wait and wait and watch it coming, and it's a damp fish." She had laughed and laughed, helplessly nearing hysteria, then brushed a dismissive kiss on Sam's wrist and fell into a separate sleep, smiling with some uncertain air of victory.

Now she ran a finger lightly along Charles's nose. "Did any of that mean anything to you—the Left?"

"I was studying music in the thirties."

"How wonderful. Just studying music."

"I had enough to do just organizing my days. But I was always sympathetic. But what could I have done about anything? Some friends took me out to a picket line at Columbia once. I can't recall the issue, but I was more of a nuisance to them than anything else; my dog hated walking around and around." He turned and kissed her nose. "You make it all sound such a waste. Was it, you think?"

"I don't know yet. When I think of the writers we all thought were so important, and no one knows their names anymore. I mean the militant people. That whole literature simply dribbled away. Gone."

"It was a style, wasn't it? Most styles crack up and disappear."

"And why is that, do you think?"

"It depends. When the occasion dominates, the work tends to vanish with the occasion."

"What should dominate, then?"

"The feelings that the occasion roused in the artist. I personally believe that what lasts is what art itself causes to exist in the artist—I mean the sounds that create other sounds, or the phrases that generate new phrases. Bach wrote some wonderful piano pieces that were really meant as piano lessons, but we listen now to their spiritual qualities, now that the occasion is forgotten. The work created its own spirituality, in a sense, and this lasts."

"What are you trying to tell me?" she asked, kissing his earlobe.

"You seem to have a need to mock yourself as you were then. I don't think you should. A lot of the past is always embarrassing—if you have any sensitivity."

"Not for you, though."

"Oh, I've had plenty of moments."

"That you're ashamed of?"

He hesitated. "For a while I tried to act as though I had sight. For a long time I refused to concede. I did some boorish things. With women especially. It was terrible."

She felt she was blushing for him and could not press him. She did not want his nobility marred. Someday he might tell her. What she imagined was that he may have, in effect, blackmailed girls with his handsome blindness, pressed himself on them as a debt they owed. That would certainly embarrass him now. In fact, she was aware of how really little she knew of his life—as little as he knew of her face. "Radicals," she said, "think they want truth, but what they really long for is high-minded characters to look up to."

"Not only radicals, Janice. People have to believe in goodness." His eyelids fluttered faster when he was excited, and they did now, like birds' wings. "They're disappointed most of the time, but in some part of his beliefs every person is naive. Even the most cynical. And memories of one's naïveté are always painful. But so what? Would you rather have had no beliefs at all?"

She buried her face in his flesh. His acceptance of her, she thought, was like a tide. She had lived a life of waiting, she thought now, and the waiting had ended, the thirst for a future was not in her anymore, she was there. With a man who had never seen her. It was wonderfully odd.

With Charles she would often think back with wonder at what now seemed like thirty years of waiting. Or had the war stalled life for everyone? Nowadays there seemed to be no future at all anymore, but it was all there was in the old days. One of her permanent stinging memories was of the day she had been shopping on Thirty-fourth Street for shoes and was walking home in new high heels, pleasured by how they sensualized the shape of her legs, when her eye fell on a corner candy store newsstand with the immense headline slashed across the *Times* front page: STALIN AND HITLER IN PACT. Fink usually brought the paper home at night, and when she handed the vendor her three pennies he said, "Sam bought one this morning."

"I know. I want one."

The man shared Fink's politics. "I thought he was going to faint," he confided. "His face went white."

With her old shoes in the box under her arm, she walked down Madison to Thirty-first Street, stopping in the middle of the sidewalk to read the incredible again and again. Simply unthinkable. Stalin so much as uttering Hitler's name without snarling was like a god being discovered screwing on the floor, or farting. Yet she felt she had to find some way to continue believing in the Soviets, which after all were still the only imaginable opposite of West End Avenue, carpets, silverware, and things.

"How can it have happened?" she asked Fink over dinner at a place called Barclay's on Eighth Street, where a meal was ninety cents rather than the sixty-five next door in the University Inn. The Village was stunned. She could feel it in the restaurant. Bud Goff, the owner, normally pumped Fink for inside political information; he believed the Party had some secret key to future events. But tonight he had merely nodded when they entered, as though at a wake.

With a wink and a canny grin, Fink tapped the side of his nose, but she knew how raked his spirit was. "Don't worry, Stalin knows what he's doing; and he's not helping Hitler—he'll never supply Germany."

"But I think he is, isn't he?"

"He is not. He's just refusing to pull the French and British chestnuts out of the fire. He's been pleading with them for a pact against Hitler for five years now, and they've stalled, hoping Hitler would attack Russia. Well, he's turned the chess game around."

She quickly agreed; in some secret windblown room in her mind, she sensed that her connection to Sam depended somehow on her keeping the faith with the Soviets—they had made Russia literate and turned her lights on. To discard the Revolution meant living without the future, meant merely living now, a frighteningly bereft feeling. In that parched year-and-a-half interval, she had seen Sam Fink straining to justify the pact to her and to their friends. And when it was no longer deniable that Russian wheat and oil were actually being shipped to a Germany that was now invading France, something within her came to a halt and stood motionless behind her eyes.

Soon after, she would happen to be in Times Square the day France capitulated to the Nazis. An immense crowd had halted on Broadway and stood reading the moving headline around the Times Building. Shame gripped her heart. Fink had explained that it was an imperialist war and that Germany, now a Soviet ally, was no worse than France, and she had tried to take that to heart, but a man standing beside her, a middle-aged round fellow in his sixties, had begun to weep into his handkerchief. It was weird how she had walked from him to the corner of Forty-second and Broadway, where a front-page photo looked up at her from a newsstand, of a round-faced middle-aged man standing on the Champs Élysées, watching the Nazi cavalry parading by as it entered Paris after the French defeat, and his eyes were flooding with tears, like a beaten child's.

Trained to reason or think her way toward hope, she put things aside, neither denied nor affirmed. She lived in waiting as though for some verdict that had not yet been announced.

Suddenly she could wait no more. "Frankly, I am almost ashamed sometimes of saying I'm not anti-Soviet," she dared to declare one night at dinner.

"My darling, you don't know what the hell you are talking about." He grinned paternally.

"But, Sam, they are helping Hitler."

"The story hasn't ended yet."

Twenty-five years on, she would look back at this, one
of her emblematic conversations, aware that she had known
at the time that she was losing respect for Sam's leadership;
and how odd that it should have come about because of a
pact made ten thousand miles away!

"But shouldn't we object? Shouldn't you?" she asked.

His mouth formed a smile that to her seemed smug, and
he shook his head with unshakable pity. That was when it
happened, the first cut of hatred for him, the first sense of
personal insult. But of course she hung on, as one did in
those times, and even pretended—not only to him but to
herself—that she had absorbed another of his far-seeing
lessons.

She felt paralyzed. They went coolly to bed, with the
winds of the world crossing their faces. They knew they did
not like one another that night. But how she could love him
if he could only admit how wounded he was! Still, maybe a
marriage could more easily sustain both parties lying rather
than one. This must be a chapter for us, she thought.
Maybe now it will all change. She reached to his shoulder,
but he seemed happily asleep. Closing her eyes, she invited
Cary Grant to lean over her and speak ironically as he undid
his incredible bow tie and slipped out of his clothes.

But a year and a half later, when Hitler finally broke the
pact and attacked Russia, the Village was relaxed again, with
Fascism again the enemy. The Russians were heroic, and
Janice felt part of America once more, no longer so dread-
fully ashamed of a partnership with Hitler.

Sam Fink presented himself at the 90 Church Street navy recruitment office a week after Pearl Harbor, but with his name and his nose, he was not naval officer material—the grin on the amused face of the blond examiner, a lieutenant senior grade, was not lost on Sam, nor was its irony in this anti-Fascist war—and so he enlisted in the more democratic army. The rebuff was embarrassing but not unexpected under capitalism, when for years now so many Jewish students had been having to go to Scottish and British medical schools, turned away by the *numerus clausus* of American institutions. Sam trained first in Kentucky, then in the officers' school in Fort Sill, Oklahoma, while Janice waited in broiling-hot wooden rooming houses off-base. The war might last eight or ten years, they were saying. But of course she must not complain, considering the bombing of London and the crucifixion of Yugoslavia. Desperately fighting loneliness, she taught herself shorthand and typing just in case she never landed the editorial job she had begun to apply for at magazine offices and publishing houses, which were losing men to the war.

By now she was twenty-eight, and on bad nights her bored face—the face of a trim, small horse, she had decided—could bring her close to tears. Then she would take a notebook and try to write out her feelings. "It isn't that I feel positively unattractive—I know better. But that somehow I am being kept from anything miraculous happening to me, ever."

With the dimming of her love for Sam, time moved in detached patches, and she could no longer find reasons to do or not do anything. A saving miracle was becoming a less than silly idea. "Somehow, when I look at myself, the miraculous seems to be more and more possible. Or is this hot room driving me crazy?" Here in Oklahoma, deep in America, she understood that secretly she was part of nothing larger than herself, a ridiculous person. At night, awakened by a line of tanks roaring past, she would go out on the front stoop of their cottage and wave to the officers, whose upper bodies, like centaurs, stuck up out of the top portholes. The thought of the familiar faces of the ones she knew being blown apart astonished her all over again. She had never understood life, and now it was death that bewildered her. All she was sure of was that America was beautiful for fighting the wrong! When the tanks were gone, leaving behind a rain of dust sparkling in the moon rays, she stood there wondering: "Did we huddle together with one another because we each felt unwanted?" This hateful self-affront would send her more and more gratefully and often to the bottle, and with a couple of drinks she would force the worst to her lips: "He makes love like mailing a letter." And then she would flush one more of what she called her "whorish notes" down the ever-obliging toilet.

Her rage, like everything else in this wartime, was on hold for the duration. Drunk, she saw more broadly; saw herself in a sort of a secret American consensus to conceal the vileness of their true needs. The whole apple-cheeked country, was it a gigantic fraud? Or was it only the homely ones who, when all was said and done, were—had to be—unhappy and full of hate? Back inside the cottage, she sat on the lumpy mattress and thought guiltily of poor Sam on bivouac, sleeping on the wet ground out there in the dripping pinewoods, his alien self in a swamp of Deep South accents. "What an ungrateful bitch I am," she said aloud.

And falling back onto the damp pillow: "That bastard Hitler!" and swung out into sleep on her anger. Would she ever be allotted time for anything but goodness?

II

Recalling it all later, her collision with Lionel Mayer, in all its painful ordinariness, had sent her flying off the track of her old life. He and his wife, Sylvia, a left-wing organizer for the Newspaper Guild, had been their friends for years by this time, and by some miracle he had been assigned as press officer in Sam's division. That fall, ordered out on a five-day bivouac, Sam, giving up pretending that his wife was happy hanging around army camps, asked Lionel to invite her to dinner in Loveock. Janice was vaguely unnerved at the date; Lionel, with his thick black curly hair, powerful hands, and juicy sense of the outrageous—he had acting ambitions—had always seemed to be inviting her curiosity about him; she had noticed how he lost himself staring at women, and it was easy to set him to performing for her with his impudent stories and jokes. Gradually, she had realized, with some amusement, that she had some kind of control over him. With Sam gone, he invited her to dinner, and she knew at once that he wanted to make love to her. The idea sent an exciting charge of power into her, along with a deep curiosity about how he reconciled his principled nature and his shyness with his wife with this hot interest in her—until she thought of her own behavior.

She had never been alone with him in a strange place, and he was a different man over dinner, holding her hand on the table, all but offering himself in his gaze. Calculating the risk, she thought it seemed low; he would clearly not want the undoing of his marriage any more than she did hers.

"You have gray eyes," he said, with a certain hunger she found absurd and necessary.

"Two of them, yes."

He burst out laughing, relieved that ploys were no longer necessary. Walking back to the bus stop from the restaurant, they saw the Loveock Rice Hotel sign overhead, and he simply grasped her hand and steered her into the lobby. The room clerk, a stout woman listening to a radio play and eating hard-boiled eggs out of a waxed-paper wrapper, seemed to recognize Lionel, or at least to be less than surprised to see him, and absently handed him a key after hardly any talk between them. Janice's insides caved in like sand before the notion of his experience. She was delighted. If she was recognized going up the broad mahogany stairway with him, then so be it; she numbly resolved not to stop the force that was carrying her forward and out of a dead life. Lionel descended on her like an ocean wave, tumbling her, invading her, pounding her past to bits. She had forgotten what stings of pleasure lay asleep in her groin, what lifts of feeling could swamp her brain. As they rested, a sentence spread before her mind: "The key to the present is always pleasure." In the bungalow afterward, sliding back down to the bottom of her pit, she studied her sated face in the bathroom mirror and saw how slyly feminine she really was, how somber and untruthful, and she happily and sadly winked. It flickered across her mind that she felt free once more, as she had when her father died.

Kissing Sam Fink good-bye the night he sailed for England, she thought he had never looked so handsome in his uniform and his shoulder bars and his fine double-breasted trench coat. But with the holy cause so nobly glowing in his face, his eyes, his manly grin, she mournfully knew she could not go on with him for life; even at his best it would not be enough. She was a real stinker, a total fraud. He insisted she stay behind in the apartment and not accompany him to the ship. A novel gravity was in his look now: "I know I'm not right for you, but . . ."

Guilt smashed her in the face. "Oh, but you are, you are!" What a thing to say, when he might be going to his death!

"Well, maybe we'll figure it out when I come back."

"Oh, my darling . . ." She clutched him closer than she had ever wanted to before, and he kissed her hard on the mouth in a way he'd never done.

It was still difficult for him to speak, even though it might be their last moment together. "I don't want you to think I don't know what's been happening." He glanced at a wall to escape her eyes. "I just haven't taken us seriously enough—I mean in a certain sense—and I regret it. . . ."

"I understand."

"Maybe not altogether." He looked straight at her now with his valorous warm smile. "I guess I've thought of you as a partner in the Revolution, or something like that. And I've left out everything else, or almost everything. Because my one obsession has been Fascism, it's taken up all my thinking." No, dear, it's sexual fear that's done that. "But America is on the line now, not just people like me, and Hitler is finished. So if I do come back I want to start over as a couple. I mean I want to start listening to you." He grinned, blushing. "The idea of that excites the hell out of me." Appalled at herself, she knew it was hopeless with them—he was sweet and dear, but nothing would stop him from going to meetings the rest of his life, and she could not bear to be good anymore; she wanted glory. She drew his head to her lips, kissing his brow like a benediction. In death's shadow, she thought, we part in love. He let her hand slide out of his fingers and moved to the door, where he turned to look back at her one last time; romantic! She stood in their doorway watching him as he waited in the corridor for the elevator. When its door clanked open, she raised a hand and wiggled her fingers, giving him her smile and her irony. "Proud of you, soldier!" He threw her a kiss and backed into the elevator. Would he die? She threw herself onto their bed, dry-eyed, wondering who in the world she was as she filled up with love for this noble man.

He might be gone a year. Maybe two. No one knew. She registered at Hunter as a graduate student in art history. It was perfect; her good husband off to the war in the best imaginable cause, and she in New York and not some god-forsaken army camp, taking courses with Professor Oscar Kalkofsky.

The war continued its unrelenting grip on time. The "duration" calcified most decisions; nothing long-term could be started until peace came, in probably five or six years, it was thought now. Frustration was mitigated by the solace of having a ready excuse for everything undone or put off—like confronting Sam Fink with a divorce when he was off fighting in Germany and might well be sent to the Pacific for the assault on Japan.

But suddenly the Bomb settled that and everyone was coming home. But where would she find the strength to tell Sam Fink that she could not be with him anymore? She must find a job, an independence from which to address him. She walked endlessly in Manhattan, tensed, half angry, half afraid, trying to conjure up a possible career for herself, and finally one day went to see Professor Kalkofsky, to talk not about art but about her life.

Months earlier, tired of walking, she stopped by the Argosy store on lower Fifth Avenue, to get off her feet and look for something new to read, and was talking to Peter Berger, the owner's son and Sam's immediate boss, when the professor came in. Almost immediately his quiet, self-mocking smile and wry fatalism drew her in, an affectation of weariness so patently flirtatious that it amused her. And his gaze kept flicking to her calves, her best feature.

A gentle, platinum-haired giant, he sat with European academic propriety in his office one afternoon, both enormous shoes set on the floor, his pipe smoldering in his right hand, whose two crooked fingers, broken by a Nazi torturer, spoke to her of a reality the Atlantic Ocean had sterilized before it reached America. She was sure he not only was taken with her but had no thought of a future relationship; his witty eyes and unsmiling mouth, some adamance in his unspoken demand on her, and his quiet speech that day—it all seemed to be solemnly taking charge of her body. Despite his muscled bulk, there was something womanly about him; maybe, she thought, because unlike most men, he was obviously unafraid of sex.

"Is not very complicated, Mrs. Fink." She liked his not using her first name yet and hoped, if they made love, he would continue calling her Mrs. Fink in bed. "After war like this, will be necessary to combine two contradictory drives. First, how to glamorize, as you say, cooperative modes in new society; at same time, incorporate pleasure ethic which certainly must sweep world after so much deprivation. That means following: to take what is offered, ask for it if it is not offered, regret nothing. The regret element is main thing; once you accept that you have chosen to be as you are, incredible as that seems, then regret is impossible. We have been slaves to this war and to Fascism. If Communism is brought to Poland and Europe, it will never last long in countries of the Renaissance. So now we are free, the slavery is finished, or will soon be. We are going to have to learn how to select self, and so to be free."

She had read existentialist philosophy but had never been seduced by it before, armed as she was by the decade of puritanical Marxism that followed the disgraced Jazz Age of her father. But there was another fascination: Europeans liked talking about submerged connecting themes rather than mere disjointed events, and she loved this, thinking she might figure herself out if she could only generalize with precision. But it never quite happened. As though she had known him a long time—which in a way she had—she began telling about her life. "I realize I don't have any kind of standard look, but . . ." He did not interrupt with a reassuring false compliment, and this meant he accepted her exactly as she was. This thrilled her with sudden possibilities. "But I . . . I forgot what I was starting to say." She laughed, her head full of lights, admitting a hunger for something to happen between them beyond speech.

"I think what you are saying is that you don't feel you have ever really made a choice in life."

Of course! How could he possibly have known that? She was drifting with no real goal. . . . She felt her hair, suddenly believing it must be tangled.

And he said, "I know it because I see how much expectation there is in you." Yes, that was it! "Almost any suffering is tolerable provided you have chosen it. I was in

London when they attacked Poland, but I knew I must go back, and I also knew the danger if I did. When he broke my fingers, I understood why the Church was so strong— it was built by men who had chosen to suffer for it. My pain was also chosen, and that dimension of choice, you see, made it significant; it was not wasted, not nothing."

Then he simply reached out over the arm of his chair and gripped her hand and drew her to him and meditatively kissed her lips, closing his eyes as though she symbolized something for him and his wise European suffering. She immediately knew what the years-long aching in her really was—simply that she had never truly chosen Sam, he had kind of happened to her because—yes, because she had never thought of herself like this, as a woman of value choosing to grant herself. He slipped his hand into her clothing, and even the cynicism of his cool expertise pleased her with its brazen consciousness.

She looked down at him kneeling on the floor, with his face buried between her thighs. "I love knowing what I'm doing, don't you?" she said, and laughed.

His face was broad and very white, its bones thick and strong. He looked up at her and, making a wry mouth, said, "The postwar era begins." But he kept it wry, just this side of laughter. What delight that, as she knew now, she meant nothing to him!

III

After Sam's return in September, whole guilty months passed before she could dare to tell him that she could no longer bear her life with him. It came about by accident.

Bringing it up had been difficult because he behaved

once again as though they had never had a problem; and it didn't help that somewhere in him he was taking a substantial amount of credit for destroying Fascism. His prophetic Marxism had proved itself in Russia's new postwar power and Fascism's extinction and set him consciously as a participant in history, and nobly at that. A new note, something close to arrogance, a quality she had formerly wished for him, irritated her now that their spirits had parted. But what set her off was his implying one evening that he had forced himself on a German farm woman who had given him shelter in a rainstorm one night.

She grinned, fascinated. "Tell me about it. Was she married?"

"Oh, sure. The husband was gone; she thought he'd been captured or killed at Stalingrad."

"How old was she—young?"

"About thirty, thirty-two."

"Good-looking?"

"Well, kind of heavy." In his gruff laugh she saw that he had probably decided not to be obsequious with her anymore. His lovemaking since his return had been markedly overbearing but no less inept than before; he was better at handling her body, but her feelings seemed to have no space in his mind.

"And what happened? Tell me."

"Well, Bavaria . . . We were stuck in this half-bombed-out town hall with the wind blowing through the windows, and I had a cold that was killing me. Coming into town, I'd noticed this house half a mile or so off down the road, and it'd looked tight and had smoke coming out of the chimney. So I went over. She gave me some soup. She was too stupid to hide the Nazi flag hanging over her husband's picture.

And it got late and I . . ." He pursed his lips cutely, stretched out his legs, and clasped his hands behind his head. "You really want to hear this?"

"Come on, dear, you know you want to tell it."

"Okay. I said I wanted to spend the night, and she showed me to this tiny cold room near the kitchen. And I said, 'Look, you Nazi bitch, I am sleeping in the best bed in this house. . . .' "

She laughed excitedly. "That's wonderful. And what did she do?"

"Well, she let me have her and her husband's bedroom." He left it at that.

She sensed the gap and grinned broadly. "And? Come on, what happened!" He was blushing, but pridefully. "Was she hot stuff or what? Come on! She grab for you?"

"Not at all. She was a real Nazi."

"You mean you raped her?"

"I don't know if you'd call it rape," he said, clearly hoping she would.

"Well, did she want to or not?"

"What's the difference? It wasn't all that bad."

"And how long'd you stay with her?"

"Just two nights, till we pulled out."

"And was she anti-Nazi by then?" She grinned at him. "I didn't ask."

His pride in it filled her with wonder, and release. "And did she have blond braids and a dirndl?"

"Not a dirndl."

"But blond braids?"

"As a matter of fact, yes."

"And big breasts?"

"Well, it was Bavaria," he said before he could catch

himself, and they both burst out laughing. At the moment she did not know why, but suddenly now she was free, free of him, free of her past, of the Revolution, of every last unwilling obligation. She felt a happiness as she got up and walked to his chair and bent over and kissed his tonsure. He looked up at her with love and pride in his having scaled an inhibition, and she felt pain for his awkwardness, which she saw would never leave him. He was completed now, would not go beyond his present bounds.

"I'm leaving you, Sam," she said, a touch of humor still in her voice. Suddenly she no longer had to reach down to sustain him. He would be all right.

After his disbelief, his shock and anger, she said, "You'll be fine, dear." She made a martini and crossed her legs under her on the couch as though for a nice chat. How excellent not to need anyone anymore, not to feel either pulled or repulsed; suddenly there was time simply to be interested in him.

"But where will you go?" Truly, it was as though with a face like hers he was her only harbor in the world.

The insult was even worse because he was unaware of it, and she instantly raged at the time she had wasted with him. She had developed a way of chuckling softly when hurt, tucking in her chin and looking up at her opponent with raised eyebrows and then unwinding her ironies as off a spool of wire. "Well, now that you mention it, it would hardly matter where I went, since to all intents and purposes I am nowhere now." She waited an instant. "Don't you think so, Sam?"

IV

In its seedy Parisian ornateness, the Crosby Hotel on Seventy-first off Broadway was still fairly decent then, at the end of the war, and it was wonderful to have a room with nothing in it of her own. How great to have no future! Free again. It reminded her a little of the Voltaire on the quay in '36, with her father in the next room tapping on the wall to wake her for breakfast. She dared to call Lionel Mayer—"I wondered if you needed any typing done"—and bantered with him on the phone like a teenager, dangling herself before him and taking it all back when pressed; clearly, with no war to direct his life, he was as lost as she was, a deeply unhappy young man posing as a *paterfamilias*, and soon he was standing with crotch pressed against her head as she sat typing an article he had written for *Collier's* on his Philippine experiences. But she had no illusions, or the merest inevitable ones that lasted only while he was in her, and when she was alone her emptiness ached and she felt fear for herself, passing thirty now, with no one at all.

Herman came one afternoon to see how she lived. He had lost some weight. "No more trains; I fly now. I'm buying in Chicago—you can pick up half the city for beans." He sat glancing out disapprovingly at upper Broadway. "This is a dump, sister; you picked a real good dump to waste your life in. What was wrong with Sam, too intellectual? I thought you liked intellectuals. Why don't you come in with me? We form a company, the cities are full of great buys, we can put down ten, fifteen percent and own a building, get mortgages to fix it up, raise the rents as high as you want, and walk away with fifty percent on your money."

"And what happens to the people living in those buildings?"

"They start paying a decent rent or go where they can afford. It's economics, Janice. The country is off welfare, we're moving into the biggest boom there ever was, 1920s all over again. Get on board and get out of this dump." He had eyeglasses now, when he remembered to wear them. He put them on to show her. "I'm turning thirty-six, baby, but I feel terrific. How about you?"

"I expect to feel happy, but I'm not terrific yet. But you can't have my money to throw people out on the street. Sorry, dear." She wanted to change stockings, still wore silk despite the new nylons, which felt clammy to her. Starting to open a drawer in the old dresser, she felt the pull come off in her hand.

"How can you live in this dump, everything falling apart?"

"I like everything falling apart; it's less competition for when I start falling apart."

"By the way, you never found those ashes, did you."

"What brings that up?"

"I don't know, I was just reminded because it was his birthday last August." He scratched his heavy leg and glanced again out the window. "He'd have given you the same advice. People with heads are going to be millionaires in the next five years. Real estate in New York is undervalued, and there's thousands walking around looking for decent apartments. I need somebody with me I can trust. By the way, what do you do all day? I mean it, you have a funny look to me, Janice. You look like your mind is not concentrated anymore. Am I wrong?"

She rolled a stocking up her leg, careful to keep the seam

straight."I don't want my mind concentrated, I want it receptive to what's around me. Does that seem odd or dishonorable? I'm trying to find out what I have to do to live like a person. I read books, I read philosophical novels like Camus and Sartre, and I read dead poets like Emily Dickinson and Edna St. Vincent Millay, and I also—"

"It doesn't look to me like you have any friends. Do you?"

"Why? Do friends leave traces? Maybe I'm not ready to have friends. Maybe I'm not fully born yet. Hindus believe that, you know—they think we go on being born and reborn right through life, or something like that. Life is very painful to me, Herman."

Tears had flowed into her eyes. This ridiculous person was her brother, the last one in the world she would think of confiding in, yet she trusted him more than anyone she had known, as ludicrous and overweight as he still was. She sat on the bed and saw him by the slanting gray light through the dirty window, a young blob full of plans and greed's happiness.

"I love this city," she said, with no special point in mind. "I know there are ways to be happy in it, but I haven't found any. But I know they're there." She went to the other front window and parted the dusty lace curtain and looked down at Broadway. She could smell the soot on the window. A light drizzle had begun to fall.

"I'm buying a new Cadillac."

"Aren't they awfully big? How can you drive them?"

"Like silk. You float. They're fantastic. We're trying to have a baby again; I don't want a car that joggles her belly."

"Are you really as confident as you seem?"

"Absolutely. Come in with me."

"I don't think I want to be that rich."

"I think you're still Communistic."

"I guess so. There's something wrong, living for money. I don't want to start."

"At least get out of those bonds and get into the market. You're literally losing money every hour."

"Am I? Well, I don't feel it, so the hell with it."

He heaved up onto his feet and buttoned his blue jacket, pulled his tie down, picked his topcoat off the back of a chair. "I will never understand you, Janice."

"That makes two of us, Herman."

"What are you going to do the rest of the day? I mean just as an instance."

"An instance of what?"

"Of what you do with your days."

"They play old movies on Seventy-second Street; I may go there. There's a Garbo, I think."

"In the middle of a working day."

"I love being in the movies when it's drizzling out."

"You want to come home with me for dinner?"

"No, dear. It might jiggle her belly." She laughed and quickly kissed him to take the sting out of that remark, which she had been as unprepared for as he. But in truth she did not want children, ever.

"What do you want out of life, do you know?"

"Of course I know."

"What?"

"A good time."

He shook his head, baffled. "Don't get in trouble," he said as he left.

V

She adored Garbo, anything she played in, could sit through two showings of even the most wooden of her films, which released her irony. She loved to be set afloat and pushed out to sea by these creakingly factitious Graustarkian tales, and their hilarious swan-shaped bathtubs and eagle-head faucets, their dripping Baroque doors and windows and drapes. Nowadays their glorious vileness of taste cheered her to the point of levitation, of hysteria, cut her free of all her education, rejoined her with her country. It made her want to stand on a roof and scream happily at the stars when the actress emerged from a noble white Rolls without ever catching a heel on a filmy long dress. And how unspeakably glorious Garbo's languorous "relaxing" on a chaise, the world-weariness of her yard-long pauses as she moodily jousted with her leading men—Janice sometimes had to cover her face so as not to look as Garbo gave her ceramic eyelids permission to pleasurably close at Barrymore's long-delayed kiss. And of course Garbo's cheekbones and the fabulous reflectiveness of her perfect white skin, the carved planes of her face—the woman was proof of God. Janice could lie for half an hour on her hotel bed, facing the ceiling, hardly blinking as the Garbo face hung over her eyes. She could stand before her dressing table mirrors, which cut her off at the neck, and find her body surprisingly ready and alive with a certain flow, especially from a side view, which emphasized her good thighs.

VI

The creaky elevator door opened one afternoon and she saw standing before it a handsome man in his forties, or possibly his early fifties, with a walking stick in one hand and a brief-case in the other. With an oddly straight-backed walk, he entered the elevator, and Janice only realized he was blind when he stopped hardly six inches from her and then turned himself to face the door by lifting his feet slightly instead of simply swiveling about. There was a shaving cut on his chin.

"Going down, aren't we?"

"Yes, down." Her chest contracted. A freedom close by, a liberation swept her up as for one instant he stared sightless into her face.

At the lobby, he walked straight out and across the tiled floor to the glass doors to the street. She hung on behind him and quickly came around to push the doors open for him. "May I help you?"

"Don't bother. But thanks very much."

He walked into the street, turning directly right toward Broadway, and she hurried to come up alongside him. "Do you go to the subway? I mean, that's where I'm going, if you'd like me to stay with you."

"Oh, that'd be fine, yes. Thank you, although I can make it myself."

"But as long as I'm going too . . ."

She walked beside him, surprised by his good pace. What life in his fluttering eyelids! It was like walking with a sighted man, but the freedom she felt alongside him was bringing tears of happiness to her eyes. She found herself pouring all her feeling into her voice, which suddenly flew out of her mouth with all the open innocence of a young girl's.

His voice had a dry flatness, as though not often used. "Have you lived in the hotel long?"

"Since March." And added without a qualm, "Since my divorce." He nodded. "And you?"

"Oh, I've been there for five years now. The walls on the twelfth floor are just about soundproof, you know."

"You play an instrument?"

"The piano. I'm with Decca, in the Classical division; I listen to a lot of recordings at home."

"That's very interesting." She felt his pleasure in this nice conversation without tension, she could sense his gratitude for her company as they walked. He must be lonely. People probably avoided him or were too formal or apologetic. But she had never felt more sure of herself or as free in dealing with a strange person, and for a moment she celebrated her instinct.

At the top of the subway steps she took his arm with a light grasp, as though he were a bird she might scare off. He did not resist and at the turnstile insisted on paying her fare out of a handful of nickels he had ready. She had no idea where he was going or where she could pretend to be going.

"How do you know where to get off?"

"I count the stops."

"Oh, of course; how stupid."

"I go to Fifty-seventh."

"That's where I'm going."

"You work around there?"

"Actually, I'm kind of still settling in. But I'm on the lookout for something."

"Well, you shouldn't have a problem; you seem very young."

"Actually, I wasn't really going anywhere. I just wanted to help you."

"Really."

"Yes."

"What's your name?"

"Janice Sessions. What's yours?"

"Charles Buckman."

She wanted to ask if he was married, but clearly he couldn't be, must not be; something about him was deeply self-organized and not hostage to anything or anyone.

Out on the street, he halted at the curb facing uptown. "I go to the Athletic Club on Fifty-ninth."

"May I walk with you?"

"Certainly. I work out for an hour before the office."

"You look very fit."

"You should do it. Although I think you're fit too."

"Can you tell?"

"The way you put your feet down."

"Really!"

"Oh yes, that tells a lot. Let me have your hand."

She quickly put her left hand in his right. He pressed her palm with his index and middle fingers, then pressed the heel of her thumb, and let her hand go. "You're in pretty good shape, but it would be a good thing to swim; your wind isn't very great."

She felt embraced by the sweep of his uncanny knowledge of her. "Maybe I will." She hated exercise but vowed to begin as soon as she could. Under the gray canopy of the Athletic Club, he slowed to a halt and faced her, and for the first time she could look for more than an instant past his flickering lids directly into his brown eyes. She felt she would choke with amazed gratitude, for he was smiling slightly as though pleased to be seen looking so intimately at her in this very public place. She felt herself standing more erectly than she ever had since she was born.

"I'm in 1214 if you'd like to come up for a drink."

"I'd love it." She laughed at her instantaneous acceptance. "I must tell you," she said, and heard herself with a terror of embarrassment but resolved not to quail before the need exploding in herself. "You've made me incredibly happy."

"Happy? Why?"

He was beginning to blush. It amazed her that embarrassment could penetrate his nearly immobile face.

"I don't know why. You just have. I feel you know me better than anyone ever has. I'm sorry I'm being so silly."

"No, no. Please, be sure to come tonight."

"Oh, I will."

She felt she could stretch up and kiss his lips and that he wouldn't mind, because she was beautiful. Or her hand was.

"You can turn off the light, if you like."

"I don't know. Maybe I'd rather leave it on."

He slipped out of his shorts and felt for the bed with his shin and lay down beside her as she stared into his sightless face. His hand discovered her good happy body. It was pure touch, pure truth beyond speech, everything she was was moving through his hand like water unfrozen. She was free of her whole life and kissed him hard and tenderly, praying that there was a God who would keep her from error with him, and moved his hands where she wished them to be, mastering him and enslaving herself to his slightest movements.

In a respite, he ran his fingers over her face and she held her breath, hearing his breaths suspending as he felt the curve of her nose, her long upper lip and forehead, lightly pressed her cheekbones—discovering, she was sure, that they lacked distinction and were buried in a rounded yet tightened face.

"I am not beautiful," she asked more than stated.

"You are, where it matters to me."

"Can you picture me?"

"Very well, yes."

"Is it really all right?"

"What earthly difference can it possibly make to me?" He rolled over on top of her, placing his mouth on hers, then, moving over her face, he read it with his lips. His pleasure poured into her again.

"I will die here, my heart will stop right here under you, because I don't need any more than this and I can't bear it."

"I like your lisp."

"Do you? It doesn't sound childish?"

"It does; that's why I like it. What color is your hair?"

"Can you imagine colors?"

"I think I can imagine black; is it black?"

"No, it's kind of chestnut, slightly reddish chestnut, and very straight. It falls almost to my shoulders. My head is large and my mouth is on the large side too and slightly prognathous. But I walk nicely, maybe beautifully if you ask some people. I love to walk in a sexy way."

"Your ass is wonderfully shaped."

"Yes, I forgot to mention that."

"It thrilled me to hold it."

"I'm glad." Then she added, "I'm really dumbfoundedly glad."

"And how do I look to you?"

"I think you're a splendidly handsome man. You have darkish skin and brown hair parted on the left, and a nicely shaped strong chin. Your face is kind of rectangular, I guess, kind of reassuring and silent. You are about three or four inches taller than me and your body is slim but not skinny. I think you are spectacular-looking."

He chuckled and rolled off her. She held his penis. "And this is perfection." He laughed and kissed her lightly. Then quietly he fell asleep. She lay beside him not daring to stir and wake him to life and its dangers.

In the late seventies, living in the Village, she read in the papers that the Crosby Hotel was being demolished for a new apartment house. She was working as a volunteer now for a civil rights organization, monitoring violations East and West, and decided to take an extra hour after lunch and go uptown to see the old hotel once more before it vanished. She was into her sixties now, and Charles had died in his sleep a little more than a year earlier. She came out of the subway and walked down the side street and found that the top floor, the twelfth, was already gone. Comically gone, as a matter of fact; the cube where Charles had carefully judged Mozart, Schubert, and Beethoven recordings was now open blue sky. She leaned against a building up the street from the hotel and watched the men prizing apart the brick walls with surprising ease. So it was more or less only gravity that held buildings up! She could see inside rooms, the different colors people had so carefully selected to paint the walls, what care had been taken to select the right shade! With each falling chunk of masonry, billowing bursts of dust rushed upward into the air. Each generation takes part of the city away, like ants tugging twigs. Soon they would be reaching her old room. An empty amazement crept over her. Out of sixty-one years of life, she had had fourteen good ones. Not bad.

She thought of the dozens of recitals and concerts, the dinners in restaurants, the utterness of Charles's love and reliance on her, who had become his eyes. In a way he had turned her inside out, so that she looked out at the world instead of holding her breath for the world to look at her and disapprove. She walked up closer to the front doors of the hotel and stood there across the street, catching the haunted earth-cold smell of a dying building, trying to re-capture that first time she had walked out with him into the street and then down to the subway, the last day of her homeliness. She had bought a new perfume, and it floated up to her through the dusty air and pleased her.

She turned back to Broadway and strolled past the fruit stands and the debris of collisions lying on the curbs, the broken pizza crusts of the city's eaters-in-the-streets, fruit peels and cores, a lost boot and a rotted tie, a woman sitting on the sidewalk combing her hair, the black boys ranting after a basketball, the implosion of causes, emergencies, purposes that had swept her up and which she could no longer find the strength to call back from the quickly dis-appearing past. And Charles, arm in arm with her, walking imperturbably through it all with his hat flat straight on his head and his crimson muffler wrapped neatly around his throat and whistling softly yet so strongly the mighty main theme of *Harold in Italy*. "Oh Death, oh Death," she said almost aloud, waiting on the corner for the light to change as a teenage drug dealer slowly rolled his new BMW past with its rap music defiantly blasting her face. She crossed as the light turned green, filling with wonder at her fortune at having lived into beauty.

FAME

SEVEN HUNDRED AND FIFTY thousand dollars—minus the ten percent commission, that left him six hundred and seventy-five thousand, spread over ten years. Coming out of his agent's building onto Madison Avenue, he almost smiled at this slight resentment he felt at having to pay Billy the seventy-five thousand. A gaunt, good-looking woman smiled back at him as she passed; he did not turn, fearing she would stop and begin the conversation that by now was unbearable for him. "I only wanted to tell you that it's really the wisest and funniest play I think I've ever . . ." He kept close to the storefronts as he walked, resolving once again to develop some gracious set of replies to these people, who after all—at least some of them—were sincere. But he knew he would always stand there like an oaf, for some reason ashamed and yet happy.

A rope of pearls lay on black velvet in the window of a jewelry store; he paused. My God, he thought, I could buy that! I could buy the whole window maybe. Even the store! The pearls were suddenly worthless. In the glass he saw his hound's eyes, his round, sad face and narrow beard, his sloping shoulders and wrinkled corduroy lapels; for the King of Broadway, he thought, you still look like a failure. He moved on a few steps, and a hand grasped his forearm with annoying proprietary strength and turned him to an immense chest, a yachtsman's sunburned face with a chic, narrow-brimmed hat on top.

"You wouldn't be Meyer Berkowitz?"

"No. I look like him, though."

The man blushed under his tan, looked offended, and walked away.

Meyer Berkowitz approached the corner of Fiftieth Street, feeling the fear of retaliation. What do I want them to do, hate me? On the corner he paused to study his watch. It was only a quarter to six, and the dinner was for seven-fifteen. He tried to remember if there was a movie house in the neighborhood. But there wouldn't be time for a whole movie unless he happened to come in at the beginning. Still, he could afford to pay for half a movie. He turned west on Fiftieth. A couple stared at him as he passed. His eye fell on a rack of magazines next to the corner newsstand. The edge of *Look* showed under *Life*, and he wondered again at all the airplanes, kitchen tables, dentists' offices, and trains where people would be staring at his face on the cover. He thought of shaving his beard. But then, he thought, they won't recognize me. He smiled. I am hooked. So be hooked, he muttered, and, straightening up, he resolved to admit to the next interloper that he was in fact Meyer Berkowitz and happy to meet his public. On a rising tide of honesty, he remembered the years in the Burnside Memorial Chapel, sitting beside the mummified dead, his notebooks spread on the cork floor as he constructed play after play, and the mirror in the men's room where he would look at his morose eyes, wondering when and if they would ever seem as unique as his secret fate kept promising they would someday be. On Fifth Avenue, so clean, gray, and rich, he headed downtown, his hands clasped behind his back. Two blocks west, two blocks to the right of his shoulder, the housemen in two theaters were preparing to turn the lights on over his name; the casts of two plays were at home, checking their watches; in all, maybe thirty-five people, including the stage managers and assistants, had been joined together by him, their lives changed and in a sense commanded by his words. And in his heart, in a hollowed-out place, stood a question mark: Was it possible to write another play? Thankfully he thought of his wealth again, subtracted ten percent commission from the movie purchase price of *I See You* and divided the remainder over ten years, and angrily swept all the dollars out of his head. A cabdriver slowed down beside him and waved and yelled, "Hey, Meyer!" and the two passengers were leaning forward to see him. The cab was keeping pace with him, so he lifted his left hand a few inches in a cripped wave—like a prizefighter, it occurred to him. An unexplainable disgust pressed him toward a sign overhanging the sidewalk a few yards ahead.

He had a vague recollection of eating in Lee Fong's years ago with Billy, who had been trying unsuccessfully to get him a TV assignment ("Meyer, if you would only follow a plotline . . ."). It would probably be empty at this hour, and it wasn't elegant. He pushed open the bright-red lacquered door and thankfully saw that the bar was empty and sat on a stool. Two girls were alone in the restaurant part, talking over teacups. The bartender took his order without any sign of recognizing him. He settled both arms on the bar, purposefully relaxing. The Scotch and soda arrived. He drank, examining his face, which was segmented by the bottles in front of the mirror. Cleanly and like a soft blow on his shoulder, the realization struck him that it was getting harder and harder to remember talking to anyone as he used to last year and all his life before his plays had opened, before he had come on view. Even now in this empty restaurant he was already expecting a stranger's voice behind him, and half wanting it. Crummy. A longing rose up to him to face someone with his mind on something else; someone who would not show that charged, distorted pressure in the eyes which, he knew, meant that the person was seeing his printed face superimposed over his real one. Again he watched himself in the mirror behind the bar: Meyer the Morose, Sam Ugly, but a millionaire with plays running in five countries. Setting his drink down, he noticed the soiled frayed cuffs on his once-tan corduroy jacket, and the shirt cuff sticking out with the button off. A distant feeling of alarm; he realized that he was meeting his director and producer and their wives at the Pavillon and that these clothes, to which he had never given any thought, would set him off as a character who went around like a bum when he had two hits running.

Thank God anyway that he had never married! To come home to the old wife with this printed new face—not good. But now, how would he ever know whether a woman was looking at him or at "Meyer Berkowitz" in full color on the magazine cover? Strange—in the long memorial chapel nights he had envisaged roomfuls of girls pouring over him when his plays succeeded, and now it was almost inconceivable to make a real connection with any women he knew. He summoned up their faces, and in each he saw calculation, that look of achievement. It was exhausting him, the whole thing. Months had gone by since he had so much as made a note. What he needed was an apartment in Bensonhurst or the upper Bronx somewhere, among people who . . . But they would know him in the Bronx. He sipped his second drink. His stomach was empty and the alcohol went straight to the back of his eyes, and he felt himself lifted up and hanging restfully by the neck over the bar.

The bartender, a thin man with a narrow mustache and only faint signs of Chinese features, stood before him. "I beggin' you pardon. Excuse me?"

Meyer Berkowitz raised his eyes, and before the bartender could speak, he said, "I'm Meyer Berkowitz."

"Ha!" The bartender pointed into his face with a long fingernail. "I know. I recognizin' you! On *Today* show, right?"

"Right."

The bartender now looked over Meyer's head toward someone behind him and, pointing at Meyer, nodded wildly. Then, for some reason whispering into Meyer's ear, he said, "The boss invite you to havin' something on the house."

Meyer turned around and saw a Chinese with sunglasses on standing beside the cash register, bowing and gesturing lavishly toward the expanse of the bar. Meyer smiled, nodded with aristocratic graciousness as he had seen people do in movies, turned back to the bartender and ordered another Scotch, and quickly finished the one in his hand. How fine people really were! How they loved their artists! Shit, man, this is the greatest country in the world.

He stirred the gift Scotch, whose ice cubes seemed just a little clearer than the ones he had paid for. How come his refrigerator never made such clear ice cubes? Vaguely he heard people entering the restaurant behind him. With no warning he was suddenly aware that three or four couples were at the bar alongside him and that in the restaurant part the white linen tablecloths were now alive with moving hands, plates, cigars. He held his watch up to his eyes. The undrunk part of his brain read the time. He'd finish this drink and amble over to the Pavillon. If he only had a pin for his shirt cuff . . .

"Excuse me . . ."

He turned on the stool and faced a small man with very fair skin, wearing a gray-checked overcoat and a gray hat and highly polished black shoes. He was a short, round man, and Meyer realized that he himself was the same size and even the same age, just about, and he was not sure suddenly that he could ever again write a play.

The short man had a manner, it was clear, the stance of a certain amount of money. There was money in his pause and the fit of his coat and a certain ineffable condescension in his blue eyes, and Meyer imagined a woman, no doubt the man's wife, also short, wrapped in mink, waiting a few feet away in the crowd at the bar, with the same smug look.

After the pause, during which Meyer said nothing, the short man asked, "Are you Meyer Berkowitz?"

"That's right," Mayer said, and the alcohol made him sigh for air.

"You don't remember me?" the short man said, a tiny curl of smile on the left edge of his pink mouth.

Meyer sobered. Nothing in the round face stuck to any part of his memory, and yet he knew he was not all this drunk. "I'm afraid not. Who are you?"

"You don't remember me?" the short man asked with genuine surprise.

"Well, who are you?"

The man glanced off, not so much embarrassed as un- used to explaining his identity; but swallowing his pride, he looked back at Meyer and said, "You don't remember Bernie Gelfand?"

Whatever suspicion Meyer felt was swept away. Clearly he had known this man somewhere, sometime. He felt the debt of the forgetter. "Bernie Gelfand. I'm awfully sorry, but I can't recall where. Where did I know you?"

"I sat next to you in English four years? De Witt Clinton!"

Meyer's brain had long ago drawn a blind down on all his high-school years. But the name Gelfand did rustle the fallen leaves at the back of his mind. "I remember your name, ya, I think I do."

"Oh, come on, guy, you don't remember Bernie Gelfand with the curly red hair?" With which he raised his gray felt hat to reveal a shiny bald scalp. But no irony showed in his eyes, which were transported back to his famous blazing hair and to the seat he had had next to Meyer Berkowitz in high school. He put his hat back on again.

"Forgive me," Meyer said, "I have a terrible memory. I remember your name, though."

Gelfand, obviously put out, perhaps even angered but still trying to smile, and certainly full of intense sentimental interest, said, "We were best friends."

Meyer laid a beseeching hand on Gelfand's gray coat sleeve. "I'm not doubting you, I just can't place you for the moment. I mean, I believe you." He laughed.

Gelfand seemed assuaged now, nodded, and said, "You don't look much different, you know? I mean, except for the beard, I'd know you in a minute."

"Yeah, well . . ." Meyer said, but still feeling he had offended, he obediently asked, "What do you do?" preparing for a long tale of success.

Gelfand clearly enjoyed this question, and he lifted his eyebrows to a proud peak. "I'm in shoulder pads," he said.

A laugh began to bubble up in Meyer's stomach; Gelfand's coat was in fact stiffly padded at the shoulders. But in an instant he remembered that there was a shoulder-pad industry, and the importance which Gelfand attached to his profession killed the faintest smile on Meyer's face. "Really," he said with appropriate solemnity.

"Oh, yes. I'm general manager, head of everything up to the Mississippi."

"Don't say. Well, that's wonderful." Meyer felt great relief. It would have been awful if Gelfand had been a failure—or in charge of New England only. "I'm glad you've done so well."

Gelfand glanced off to one side, letting his achievement sink deeply into Meyer's mind. When he looked again at Meyer, he could not quite keep his eyes from the frayed cuffs of the corduroy jacket and the limp shirt cuff hanging out. "What do *you* do?" he asked.

Meyer looked into his drink. Nothing occurred to him. He touched his finger against the mahogany bar and still nothing came to him through his shock. His resentment was clamoring in his head; he recognized it and greeted it. Then he looked directly at Gelfand, who in the pause had grown a look of benevolent pity. "I'm a writer," Meyer said, and watched for the publicity-distorted freeze to grip Gelfand's eyeballs.

"That so!" Gelfand said, amused. "What kind of writing you do?"

If I really had any style, Meyer thought, I would shrug and say I write part-time poems after I get home from the post office, and would leave Bernie to enjoy his dinner. On the other hand, I do not work in the post office, and there must be some way to shake this monkey off and get back to where I can talk to people again as if I were real. "I write plays," he said to Gelfand.

"That so!" Gelfand smiled, his amusement enlarging toward open condescension. "Anything I would have . . . heard of?"

"Well, as a matter of fact, one of them is down the street."

"Really? On *Broadway?*" Gelfand's face split into its parts; his mouth still kept its smile, but his eyes showed a certain wild alarm. His head, suddenly, was on straighter, his neck drawn back.

"I wrote *I See You*," Meyer said, and tasted slime on his tongue.

Gelfand's mouth opened. His skin reddened.

"And *Mostly Florence.*"

The two smash hits seemed to open before Gelfand's face like bursting flats. His finger lifted toward Meyer's chest. "Are you . . . *Meyer Berkowitz?*" he whispered.

"Yes."

Gelfand held out his hand tentatively. "Well, I'm very happy to meet you," he said with utter formality.

Meyer saw distance locking into place between them, and in the instant wished he could take Gelfand in his arms and wipe out the poor man's metaphysical awe, smother his defeat, and somehow retract this very hateful pleasure, which he knew now he could not part with anymore. He shook Gelfand's hand and then covered it with his left hand.

"Really," Gelfand went on, withdrawing his hand as

though it had already presumed too much. "I . . . I've enjoyed your—excuse me." Meyer's heavy cheeks stirred vaguely toward a smile.

Gelfand closed his coat and quickly turned about and hurried to the little crowd waiting for tables near the red entrance door. He took the arm of a short woman in a mink wrap and turned her toward the door. She seemed surprised as he hurried her out of sight and into the street.

FITTER'S NIGHT

By four in the afternoon it was almost dark in winter, and this January was one of the coldest on record, so that the night shift filing through the turnstiles at the Navy Yard entrance was somber, huddling in zipper jackets and pulling down earflaps, shifting from foot to foot as the marine guards inspected each tin lunchbox in turn and compared the photographs on identity cards with the squint-eyed, blue-nosed faces that passed through. The former grocery clerks, salesmen, unemployed, students, and the mysteriously incapacitated young men whom the army and navy did not want; the elderly skilled machinists come out of retirement, the former truckdrivers, elevator operators, masons, disbarred lawyers, and a few would-be poets, poured off the buses in the blue light of late afternoon and waited their turn at the end of the lines leading to the fresh-faced marines in the booths, who refused to return their quips and dutifully searched for the bomb and the incendiary pencil under the lettuce-and-tomato sandwiches leaking through the waxed paper, against all reason unscrewing the Thermos bottles to peer in at the coffee. With some ten thousand men arriving for each of the three shifts, the law of averages naturally came into play, and it was inevitable that every few minutes someone would put his Thermos back into his lunchbox and say, "What's Roosevelt got against hot coffee?" and the marines would blink and wave the joker into the Yard.

To the naval architects, the engineers, the yardmaster and his staff, the New York Naval Shipyard was not hard to define; in fact, it had hardly changed since its beginnings in the early 1800s. The vast drydocks facing the bay were backed by a maze of crooked and curving streets lined with one-story brick machine shops and storehouses. In dark Victorian offices, papers were still speared on sharp steel points, and filing cabinets were of dark oak. Ships of war were never exactly the same, whatever anybody said, and the smith was still in a doorway hammering one-of-a-kind iron fittings, the sparks falling against his floor-length apron; steel bow plates were still sighted by eye regardless of the carefully mapped curves of the drawing, and when a man was injured, a two-wheel pushcart was sent for to bump him along the cobblestones to the infirmary like a side of beef.

It was sure that *someone* knew where everything was, and this faith was adopted by every new man. The shipfitter's helper, the burner, the chipper, the welder; painters, carpenters, riggers, drillers, electricians—hundreds of them might spend the first hour of each shift asking one stranger after another where he was supposed to report or what drydock held the destroyer or carrier he had been working on the night before; and there were not a few who spent entire twelve-hour shifts searching for their particular gangs, but the faith never faltered. Someone must know what was supposed to be happening, if only because damaged ships did limp in under tow from the various oceans and after days, weeks, or sometimes months they did sail out under Brooklyn Bridge, ready once again to fight the enemy. There were naturally a sensitive few who, watching these gallant departures, shook their heads with wonder at the mystery of how these happened to have been repaired, but the vast majority accepted this and even felt that they themselves were somehow responsible. It was like a baseball game with five hundred men playing the outfield at the same time, sweeping in a mob toward the high arching ball, which was caught somewhere in the middle of the crowd, by whom no one knew, except that the game was slowly and quite inconceivably being won.

Tony Calabrese, shipfitter first class, was one of that core of men who did know where to report once he came through the turnstile at four in the afternoon. In "real life," as the phrase went, he had been a steamfitter in Brooklyn and was not confused by mobs, marines looking into his sandwiches, or the endless waiting around that was normal in a shipyard. Once through the turnstile, his lunchbox tucked under his arm again, his cap on crooked, he leaned into the wind with his broken nose, notifying oncoming men to clear the way, snug inside his pile zipper jacket and woolen shirt, putting down his feet on the outside edges like a bear, bandy-legged, low-crotched, a graduate of skyscraper construction, brewery repairing, and for eight months the city Department of Water Supply, until it was discovered that he had been sending a substitute on Tuesdays, Wednesdays, and Fridays while he went to the track and made some money.

Tony had never until a year and a half ago seen a ship up close and had no interest in ships, any more than he had had in the water supply, breweries, or skyscrapers. Work was a curse, a misfortune that a married man had to bear, like his missing front tooth, knocked out in a misunderstanding with a bookie. There was no mystery to what the good life was, and he never lived a day without thinking about it, and more and more hopelessly now that he was past forty; it was being like Sinatra, or Luciano, or even one of the neighborhood politicians who wore good suits all day and never bent over, kept two apartments, one for the family, the other for the baloney of the moment. He had put his youth into trying for that kind of life and had failed. Driving the bootleggers' trucks over the Canadian border, even a season as Johnny Peaches's bravo and two months collecting for a longshoremen's local, had put him within reach of a spot, a power position from which he might have retired into an office or apartment and worked through telephones and over restaurant tables. But at the last moment something in his makeup had always defeated him, sent him rolling back into the street and a job and a paycheck, where the future was the same never-get-rich routine. He knew he was simply not smart enough. If he were, he wouldn't be working in the Navy Yard.

His face was as round as a frying pan with a hole in it, a comical face now that the nose was flattened and his front tooth gone, and no neck. He had risen to first in a year and a half, partly because the supervisor, old Charley Mudd, liked a good phone number, which Tony could slip him, and also because Tony could read blueprints quickly, weld, chip, burn, and bulldoze a job to its finish when, as happened occasionally, Charley Mudd had to get a ship back into the war. As shipfitter first, he was often given difficult and complicated jobs and could call on any of the various trades to come in and burn or weld at his command. But he was not impressed by his standing, when Sinatra could open his mouth and make a grand. More important was that his alliance with Charley Mudd gave him jobs belowdecks in cold weather and abovedecks when the sky was clear. If indisposed, he could give Charley Mudd the sign and disappear for the night into a dark corner and a good sleep. But most of the time he enjoyed being on the job, particularly when he was asked how to perform one operation or another by "shipfitters" who could not compute a right angle or measure in smaller units than halves. His usual way of beginning his instruction was always the same and was expected by anyone who asked his help. He would unroll the blueprint, point to a line or figure, and say, "Pay 'tention, shithead," in a voice sludged with the bottom of wine bottles and the Italian cigars he inhaled. No one unable to bear this indignity asked him for help, and those who did knew in advance that they would certainly lose whatever pretensions they thought they had.

But there was another side to Tony, which came out during the waits. Before Pearl Harbor there had been some six thousand men employed in the Yard, and there were now close to sixty thousand. Naturally they would sometimes happen to collect in unmanageable numbers in a single compartment, and the repairs, which had to be done in specific stages, made it impossible for most of them to work and for any to leave. So the waits began; maybe the welder could not begin welding until the chipper finished breaking out the old weld, so he waited, with his helper or partner. The burner could not cut steel until the exhaust hose was brought down by his helper, who could not get hold of one until another burner down the corridor was finished with it, so he waited; a driller could not drill until his point was struck into the steel by the fitter, who was forbidden to strike it until the electricians had removed the electric cables on the other side of the bulkhead through which the hole had to be drilled, so they waited; until the only way out was a crap game, or Tony "enjoying" everybody by doing imitations or picking out somebody to insult and by going into his grin, which, with the open space in his teeth, collapsed the company in hysteria. After these bouts of entertainment Tony always became depressed, reminded again of his real failing, a lack of stern dignity, leadership, force. Luciano would hardly be clowning around in a cruiser compartment, showing how stupid he could look with a tooth missing.

On this January afternoon, already so dark and the wind biting at his eyes, Tony Calabrese, going down the old streets of the Yard, had decided to work belowdecks tonight, definitely. Even here in the shelter of the Yard streets the wind was miserable—what would it be like on a main deck open to the bay? Besides, he did not want to tire himself this particular shift, when he had a date at half past four in the morning. He went through his mental checklist: Dora would meet him at Baldy's for breakfast; by six A.M. he would be home to change his clothes and take a shower; coffee with the kids at seven before they went to school, then maybe a nap till nine or half past, then pick up Dora and make the first show at the Fox at ten; by twelve to Dora's room, bang-bang, and a good sleep till half past two or three, when he would stop off at home and put on work clothes, and maybe see the kids if they got home early, and into the subway for the Yard. It was a good uncomplicated day in front of him.

Coming out of the end of the street, he saw the cold stars over the harbor, a vast sky stretching out over the bay and beyond to the sea. Clusters of headlights coursed over

Brooklyn Bridge, the thickening traffic of the homebound who did not know they were passing over the Yard or the war-broken ships. He picked his way around stacks of steel plate and tarpaulin-shrouded gear piled everywhere, and for a moment was caught in the blasting white glare of the arc lamp focused downward from the top of a traveling crane; slowly, foot by foot, it rolled along the tracks, tall as a four-story building on two straddling legs, its one arm thrust out against the stars, dangling a dull glinting steel plate the width of a bus, and led by a fitter hardly taller than its wheels, who was walking backward between the tracks ahead of it and pointing off to the right in the incandescent whiteness of its one eye. As though intelligent, the crane obediently swiveled its great arm, lowering the swaying plate to a spot pointed at by the fitter, whose face Tony could not make out, shaded as it was by the peak of the cap against the downpouring light of the high white eye. Tony circled wide around the descending plate, trusting no cable or crane operator, and passed into the darkness again toward the cruiser beyond, raised in the drydock, her bow curving high over the roadway on which he walked with his lips pressed together to keep the wind off his teeth. Turning, he moved along her length, head down against the swift river of cold air, welcoming the oncoming clumps of foot-stamping men mounting her along the gangplank—the new shift boarding, the occasional greeting voice still lively in the earliness of the evening. He rocked up the length of the gangplank onto the main deck, with barely a nod passing the young lieutenant in upturned collar who stood hitting his gloved hands together in the tiny temporary guardhouse at the head of the plank. There was the happy smell of burned steel and coffee, the straightforward acridity of the navy, and the feeling of the hive as he descended a steep stair clogged down its whole length with black welders' cables and four-inch exhaust hoses, the temporary intestine that always followed repair gangs into the patient ships.

His helper, Looey Baldu—where an Italian got a name like Baldu, Tony could not understand, unless a Yugoslav had got into the woodpile or they shortened it—Looey was already waiting for him in the passageway, twenty-three, dignified and superior with his high-school education, in regulation steel-tipped shoes—which Tony steadfastly refused to wear—and giving his resolute but defensive greeting.

"Where's Charley Mudd?"

"I didn't see him yet."

"You blind? There he is."

Tony walked around the surprised Baldu and into a compartment where Charley Mudd, sixty and half asleep, sat on three coils of electric cable, his eyes shut and a clipboard starting to slide out of his opening hands. Tony touched the older man's back and bent to talk softly and put in the fix. Charley nodded, his eyes rolling. Tony gave him a grateful pat and came out into the passageway, which was filling with men trying to pass one another in opposite directions while dragging endless lengths of hose, cable, ladders, and bulky toolboxes, everybody looking for somebody else, so that Tony had to raise his voice to Baldu. He always spoke carefully to the high-school graduate, who never caught on the first time but was a good boy although his wife, he said, was Jewish. Baldu was against race prejudism, whatever the hell that meant, and frowned like a judge when talked to, as though some kind of veil hung before his face and nothing came through it loud and clear.

"We gonna watertight hatches C Deck," Tony said, and he turned, hands still clenched inside his slit pockets, and walked.

Baldu had had no time to nod and already felt offended, but he followed with peaked eyebrows behind his fitter, keeping close so as not to know the humiliation of being lost again and having to face Tony's scathing ironies implying incessant masturbation.

They descended to C Deck, a large, open area filled with tiered bunks in which a few sailors lay, some sleeping, others reading or writing letters. Tony was pleased at the nearness of the coffee smell, what with any more than a pound a week almost impossible for civilians to get except at black-market prices. Without looking again at his helper, he unzipped his jacket, stowed his lunchbox on the deck under an empty bunk, took out a blue handkerchief and blew his nose and wiped his teary eyes, removed his cap and scratched his head, and finally sat on his heels and ran his fingers along the slightly raised edge of a hatch opening in the deck, through which could be seen a ladder going down into dimness.

"Let that there cover come to me, Looey."

Baldu, his full brown-paper lunch bag still in his hand, sprang to the heavy hatch cover lying on the deck and with one hand tried to raise it on its hinges. Unwilling to admit that his strength was not enough or that he had made a mistake, he strained with the one hand, and as Tony regarded him with aggravation and lowering lids, he got the hatch cover up on one knee, and only then let his lunch bag down onto the deck and with two hands finally raised the cover toward Tony, whose both hands were poised to stop it from falling shut.

"Hold it, hold it right there."

"Hold it open?"

"Well, what the fuck, you gonna hold it closed? Of course open. What's a-matta wichoo?"

Tony felt with his fingertips along the rubber gasket that ran around the lip of the cover. Then he took hold of it and let it close over the hatch. Bending down until his cheek pressed the cold deck, he squinted to see how closely gasket met steel. Then he got up, and Looey Baldu stood to face him.

"I'm gonna give you a good job, Looey. Git some chalk, rub it on the gasket, then git your marks on the deck. Where the chalk don't show, build it up with some weld, then git a grinder and tell him smooth it nice till she's nice an' even all around. You understand?"

"Sure, I'll do it."

"Just don't get wounded. That's it for tonight, so take it easy."

Baldu's expression was nearly fierce as he concentrated patriotically on the instructions, and now he nodded sternly and started to step back. Tony grabbed him before he tripped over the hatch cover beind him, then let him go and without further remark fled toward the coffee smell.

It was going to be a pretty good night. Dora, whom he had gotten from Hindu, was a little shorter than he would have liked, but she had beautiful white skin, especially her breasts, and lived alone in a room with good heat—no sisters, aunts, mother, nothing. And both times she had brought home fresh bread from Macy's, where she packed nights. Now all he had to do was keep relaxed through the shift so as not to be sleepy when he met her for breakfast at Baldy's. Picking his way along a passage toward the intensifying coffee smell, he felt joyous, and seeing a drunken sailor trying to come down a ladder, he put his shoulder under the boy's seat and gently let him down to the deck, then helped him a few yards along the passage until the boy fell into a bunk. Then he lifted his legs onto it, turned him over, opened his pea jacket and shoelaces, and returned to the search for the source of the coffee smell.

He might have known. There was Hindu, standing over an electric brewer tended by two sailors in T-shirts. Hindu was big, but next to him stood a worker who was a head taller, a giant. Tony sauntered over, and Hindu said to the sailors, "This here's a buddy, how about it?"

A dozen lockers stood against the nearby bulkhead, from one of which a sailor took a clean cup and a five-pound bag of sugar. Tony thanked him as he took the full cup and then moved a foot away as Hindu came over.

"Where you?" Hindu asked.

"C Deck, watertight hatch cover. Where you?"

"I disappeared. They're still settin' up the windbreak on Main Deck."

"Fuck that."

"You know what Washington said when he crossed the Delaware?"

Then both together, "It's fuckin' cold."

They drank coffee. Hindu's skin was so dark he was sometimes taken for an Indian; he made up for it by keeping his thick, wavy hair well combed, his blue beard closely shaved, and his big hands clean.

"I gotta make a phone call," he said quietly, stooping to Tony. "I left her bawlin'. Jesus, I passed him comin' up the stairs."

"Ta hell you stay so long?"

"I coun' help myself." His eyes softened, his mouth worked in pleasurable agony. "She's dri'n' me crazy. We even wen' faw walk."

"You crazy?"

"I coun' help it. If you seen her you drop dead. Byoo-diful. I mean it. I'm goin' crazy. I passed him comin' up the stairs, I swear!"

"You'll end up fuckin' a grave, Hindu."

"She touches me, I die. I die. I die, Tony." Hindu shut his eyes and shook his head, memorializing.

Activity behind them turned them about. The big worker, his coffee finished, was pulling on a chain that ran through a set of pulleys hooked to a beam overhead, and a gigantic electric motor was rising up off the deck. Tony, Hindu, and the two sailors watched the massive rigger easily raise the slung motor until it reached the pulleys and could be raised no farther, with three inches yet to go before it could be slid onto a platform suspended from the deck over-head. The rigger drew his gauntlets up tighter, set himself underneath the motor with his hands up under it, and, with knees bent, pushed. The motor rose incredibly until its feet were a fraction above the platform; the rigger pushed and got it hung. Then he came out from under, stood behind it, and shoved it fully onto the platform where it belonged. His face was flushed, and, expanded by the effort, he looked bigger than ever. Slipping off his gauntlets, he looked down to the sailors, who were still sitting on the deck.

"Anybody ever read *Oliver Wiswell*?"

"No."

"You ought to. Gives you a whole new perspective on the American Revolution. You know, there's a school that doesn't think the Revolution was necessary."

Tony was already walking, and Hindu followed slightly behind, asking into his ear, "Maybe I could hang wichoo tonight, Tony. Okay? I ask Cholly, okay?"

"Go ahead."

Hindu patted Tony's back thankfully and hurried up a ladder.

Tony looked at his pocket watch. Five o'clock. He had chopped an hour. It was too early to take a nap. A sense of danger struck him, and he looked ahead up the passage, but there was only a colored worker he did not know fooling with a chipping gun that would not receive its chisel. He turned the other way in time to see a captain and a man in a felt hat and overcoat approaching with blueprints half unrolled in their hands. He caught sight of a chipping-gun air hose, which he followed into a compartment on hands and knees. The two brass went by, and he stood up and walked out of the compartment.

It was turning into one of the slow nights when the clock never moved. The coffee had sharpened him even more, so a nap was out of the question. He moved along passageways at a purposeful pace, up ladders and down, looking for guys he might know, but the ship was not being worked much tonight; why, he did not know and did not care. Probably there was a hurry-up on the two destroyers that had come in last night. One had a bow blasted off, and the other had floated in from the bay listing hard to one side. The poor bastards on the destroyers, with no room to move and some of those kids seasick in bad weather. The worst was when the British ships came in. Good he wasn't on one of those bastards, with the cockroaches so bad you couldn't sit down, let alone stretch out, and their marines a lot of faggos. That was hard to believe the first time he saw it—like last sum-

ARTHUR MILLER

mer with that British cruiser, the captain pacing the deck day and night and the ship in drydock. A real jerked-off Englishman with a monocle and a mustache and a crushed cap, and a little riding crop in his hands clasped behind his back, scowling at everybody and refusing to go off duty even in drydock. And piping whistles blowing every few hours to bring the marines on deck for rifle drill, that bunch of fags screaming through the passageways, goosing each other, and pimples all over their faces. Christ, he hated the English the way they kicked Italy around, sneering. And those stupid officers, in July, walking around in thick blue hairy uniforms, sweating like pigs all over their eyeglasses. You could tell a U.S. ship blindfolded, the smell of coffee and cleanliness, and ice water anywhere you looked. Of course they said the British gunners were better, but who was winning the war, for Christ's sake? Without us they'd have to pack it in and salute the fuckin' Germans. The French had a good ship, that captured *Richelieu*—what paneling in the wardroom, like a fuckin' palace—but something was wrong with the guns, they said, and couldn't hit nothin'.

He found himself in the engine room and looked up through the barrel-like darkness, up and up through the belly of the ship. There was, he knew, a cable passage where he could lie down. Somebody he could barely see high above in the darkness was showering sparks from a welding arc being held too far from the steel, but he pulled up his collar and climbed ladders, moved along the catwalks until he came to a low door which he opened, went into a hole lined with electric cables, and lay down with his hands clasped under his head. The welding buzz was all he could hear now. Footsteps would sound on the steel catwalks and give good warning.

[74]

Not tired, he closed his eyes to screw the government. Even here in the dark he was making money every minute —every second. With this week's check he would probably have nearly two thousand in his account and a hundred and twenty or so in the account Margaret knew about. Jesus, what a dumb woman! Dumb, dumb, dumb. But a good mother, that's for sure. But why not? With only two kids, what else she got to do? He would never sleep with her again and could barely remember the sight of her body. In fact, for the thousandth time in his life, he realized that he had never seen his wife naked, which was as it should be. You could fill a lake with the tears she had shed these fifteen years—an ocean. Good.

He stoked his anger at his wife, the resentment that held his life together. It was his cause, his agony, and his delight to let his mind go and imagine what she must feel, not being touched for eleven—no, twelve, yes, it was twelve last spring—years. This spring it would be thirteen, then fourteen, then twenty, and into her grave without his hand on her. Never, never would he give in. On the bed, when he did sleep at home, with his back to her, he stretched into good sleep, and sometimes her wordless sobs behind him were like soft rain on the roof that made him snug. She had asked for it. He had warned her at the time. He might look funny, but Tony Calabrese was not funny for real. To allow himself to break, to put his hand on her ever again, he would have to forgive what she had done to him. And now, lying in the cable passage with his eyes closed, he went over what she had done, and as always happened when he reached for these memories, the darling face of the baloney formed in his darkness, Patty Moran, with genuine red hair, breasts without a crease under them, and lips pink as lipstick. Oh, Jesus! He shook his head in the dark. And where was she now? He did not dare hate his grandfather; the old man was like a storm or an animal that did only what it was supposed to do. He let himself remember what had become for him like a movie whose end he knew and dreaded to see once more, and yet wanted to. It was the only time in his life that had not been random, when each day that had passed in those few months had changed his position and finally sealed him up forever.

From the day he was born, it seemed to him, his mother had kept warning him to watch out for Grampa. If he stole, hit, lied, tore good pants, got in cop trouble, the same promise was made—if Grampa ever came to America he would settle each and every one of Tony's crimes in a day-long, maybe weeklong beating combined with an authoritative spiritual thundering that would straighten out Tony for the rest of his life. For Grampa was gigantic, a sport in the diminutive family, a throwback to some giants of old whose wit and ferocity had made them lords in Calabria, chiefs among the rocks, commanders of fishing boats, capos of the mines. Even Tony's cowed father relied on the absent, never-seen old man for authority and spent every free hour away from work on the BMT tracks playing checkers with his cronies, rather than chastise his sons. Grampa would come one day and settle them all, straighten them out, and besides, if he did come, he would bring his money. He owned fishing boats, the star of the whole family, a rich man who had made it, astoundingly, without ever leaving Calabria, which meant again that he was wily and merciless, brave and just.

The part that was usually hard to remember was hard to remember again, and Tony opened his eyes in the cable passage until, yes, he remembered. How he had ever gotten mixed up with Margaret in the first place, a mewly girl, big-eyed but otherwise blanketed bodily, bodiless, shy, and frightened. It was because he had just come out of the Tombs, and this time Mama was not to be fooled with. She was a fury now as he walked into the tenement, unwilling to listen to the old promises or to be distracted by all his oaths of innocence and frame-up. And this time fate began to step in, that invisible presence entered Tony's life, the Story; his tight time began, when nothing was any longer random and every day changed what he was and what he had to do.

A letter had arrived that nobody could read. They sat around the table, Mama and Papa and Aunt Celia from next door, and Frank and Salvatore, his married cousins. Tony slowly traced the Italian script, speaking it aloud so that Papa could mouth the words and penetrate the underlying thought, which was unbelievable, a marvel that chilled them all. Grampa had sold his holdings, now that Grandma was dead, and was sailing for America for a visit, or, if he approved, to stay the rest of his life.

The cable passage seemed to illuminate with the lightning flashes of the preparations for the arrival—the house scrubbed, walls painted, furniture shined, chairs fixed, and the blackmail begun. Mama, seeing the face of her son and the hope and avidity in his eyes, sat him down in the kitchen. I am going to tell Grampa everything what you done, Tony. Everything. Unless you do what I say. You marry Margaret.

Margaret was a year older than Tony. Somehow, he could not imagine how, now that he knew her, he had come to rest on her stoop from time to time, mainly when just out of jail, when momentarily the strain of bargaining for life and a spot was too much, those moments when, like madness, a vision of respectability overwhelmed him with a quick longing for the clean and untroubled existence. She was like a nervous pony at his approach, and easy to calm. It was the time he was driving booze trucks over the Canadian border for Harry Ox, the last of the twenties, and out of jail it was sweet to spend a half hour staring at the street with Margaret, like a clam thrown up by the moiling sea for a moment. He had been in his first gunfight near Albany and was scared. And this was the first time he had said he would like to take her to the movies. In all the years he had known her, the thought had never crossed his mind to make a date. Home that night, he already heard his mother talking about Margaret's family. The skein was folding over him, and he did not resist. He did not decide either. He let it come without touching it, let it drape over him like a net. They were engaged, and nobody had used the word, even, but whenever he saw Margaret she acted as though she had been waiting for him, as though he had been missing, and he let it happen, walked a certain way with her in the street, touching her elbow with his fingertips, and never took her into the joints, and watched his language. Benign were the smiles in her house the few times he appeared, but he could never stay long for the boredom, the thickness of the plot to strangle his life.

His life was Patty Moran by this time. Once across her threshold over Ox's saloon, everything he saw nearly blinded him. He had started out with her at three o'clock in the morning in the back of Ox's borrowed Buick, her ankle ripping the corded rope off the back of the front seat, and the expanse of her thigh across the space between the back and front seats was painted in cream across his brain forever. He walked around the neighborhood dazed, a wire going from the back of his head to her hard soft belly. She was not even Harry Ox's girl but a disposable one among several, and Tony started out knowing that and each day climbed an agonizing stairway to a vision of her dearness, almost but not quite imagining her marriageable. The thought of other men with her was enough to bring his fist down on a table even if he was sitting alone. His nose had not yet been broken; he was small but quick-looking, sturdy and black-eyed. She finally convinced him there was nobody else, she adored his face, his body, his stolen jokes. And in the same two or three months he was taking Margaret to the movies. He even kissed her now and then. Why? Why! Grampa was coming as soon as he could clear up his affairs, and what had begun with Margaret as a purposeless yet pleasant pastime had taken on leverage in that it kept Mama pleased and quiet and would guarantee his respectability in Grampa's eyes—long enough, anyway, to get his inheritance.

No word of inheritance was written in the old man's letters, but it was first imagined, then somehow confirmed, that Tony would get it. And when he did it was off-to-Buffalo, him and the baloney, maybe even get married someplace where nobody knew her and they'd make out seriously together. And best of all, Mama knew nothing of the baloney. Nowadays she was treating Tony like the head of the house. He had taken a job longshore, was good as gold, and sat home many an evening, listening to the tock-tick.

The final letter came. Tony read it alone in the bathroom first and announced that Grampa was coming on the tenth, although the letter said the ninth. On the morning of the ninth, Tony said he had to get dressed up because, instead of working, he was going to scout around for a good present for Grampa's arrival tomorrow. Congratulated, kissed, waved off, he rounded the block to Ox's and borrowed three hundred dollars and took a cab to the Manhattan pier.

The man in truth was gigantic. Tony's first glimpse was this green-suited, oddly young old man, a thick black tie at his throat, a black fedora held by a porter beside him, while down the gangway he himself was carrying on his back a small but heavy trunk. Tony understood at once—the money was in the trunk. On the pier Tony tipped the porter for carrying the furry hat, and kissed his six-foot grandfather once he had set the trunk down. Tony shook his hand and felt the power in it, hard as a banister. The old man took one handle of the trunk and Tony the other, and in the cab Tony made his proposal. Before rushing home, why not let him show New York?

Fine. But first Tony wanted to Americanize the clothes; people would get the wrong impression, seeing such a green immigrant suit and the heavy brogans. Grampa allowed it, standing there ravished by the bills Tony peeled off for the new suit, new shoes, and an American tie. Now they toured the town, sinking deeper and deeper into it as Tony graded the joints from the middle-class ones uptown to his hangouts near Canal Street, until the old man was kissing his grandson two and three times an hour and stood up cheering the Minsky girls who bent over the runway toward his upturned face. Tony, at four in the morning, carried the trunk up the stairs of the tenement on his own back, feeling the dead weight inside; then back down and carried Grampa on his back and laid him in his own bed and himself on the floor. He had all he could do to keep from rushing over to Patty Moran to tell her he was in like Flynn, the old man loved him like a son, and they might begin by opening a joint together someplace, like in Queens. But he kept discipline and slept quickly, his face under the old man's hand hanging over the edge of the mattress.

In the cable passage, staring at the dark, he could not clearly recall his wedding, any more than he had been able to an hour after the ceremony. It was something he was doing and not doing. Grampa had emerged from the bedroom with Tony under his armpit; and seeing her father, Mama's face lengthened out as though God or the dead had walked in, especially since she had just finished getting dressed up to meet his boat. The shouting and crying and kissing lasted until afternoon, Grampa's pleasure with his manly grandson gathering the complicated force of a new mission in his life, a proof of his own grandeur at being able to hand on a patrimony to a good man of his blood, a man of style besides.

Papa nodded an uncertain assent, one eye glancing toward the trunk, but as evening came, Mama, Tony saw, was showing two thoughts in her tiny brown eyes, and after the third meal of the day, with the table cleaned off and the old man blinking drowsily, she laid two open hands on the table, smiled deferentially, and said Tony had been in and out of jails since he was twelve.

Grampa woke up.

Tony was hanging with bootleggers, refused until the last couple of months to hold a regular job, and now he was staying with an Irish whore when he had engaged himself to Margaret, the daughter of a good Calabrian family down the block, a girl as pure as a dove, beautiful, sincere, whose reputation was being mangled every day Tony avoided talk of a marriage date. The girl's brothers were growing restive, her father had gotten the look of blood in his eye. Margaret alone could save Tony from the electric chair, which was waiting for him as sure as God had sent Jesus, for he was a boy who would lie as quickly as spit, the proof being his obvious attempt to hoodwink Grampa with a night on the town before any of the family could get to him with the true facts.

It took twenty minutes to convince Grampa; he had had to stare at Tony for a long time, as though through a tele-scope that would not adjust. Tony downed his fury, de-fended his life, denied everything, promised everything, brought out the new alarm clock he had bought for the house out of his own money, and at last sat facing Grampa, dying in his chair as the old man leveled his judgment. Tony, you will marry this fine girl or none of my money goes to you. Not the fruit of my labor to a gangster, no, not to a criminal who will die young in the electric chair. Marry the girl and yes, definitely, I give you what I have.

First days, then weeks—then was it months?—passed af-ter the wedding, but the money failed to be mentioned again. Tony worked the piers dutifully now, and when he did see Patty Moran it was at odd hours only, on his way toward the shape-up or on days when it rained and deck work was called off. He would duck into the doorway next to Ox's saloon and fly up the stairs and live for half an hour, then home again to wait; he dared not simply confront the old man with the question of his reward, knowing that he was being watched for deficiencies. On Sundays he walked like a husband with Margaret, spent the afternoons with the family, and acted happy. The old man was never again as close and trusting and comradely as on that first night off the boat, but neither was he hostile. He was watching, Tony saw, to make sure.

And Tony would make him sure. The only problem was what to do in his apartment once he was alone with Margaret. He had never really hated her and he had never liked her. It was like being alone with an accident, that was all. He spoke to her rarely and quietly, listened to her gossip about the day's events, and read his newspaper. He did not expect her to suddenly stand up in the movies and run out crying, some two months after the wedding, or expect to come home from work one spring evening and find Grampa sitting in the living room with Margaret, looking at him silently as he came through the door.

You don't touch your wife?

Tony could not move from the threshold or lie, suddenly. The old man had short, bristly gray hair that stood up like wire, and he was back to his Italian brogans, a kick from which could make a mule inhale. Margaret dared only glance at Tony, but he saw now that the dove had her beak in his belly and was not going to let go.

You think I'm mentally defective, Tony? A man with spit in the corners of his mouth? Cross-eyed? What do you think I am?

The first new demonstration was, again, at the movies. Grampa sat behind them. After a few minutes Margaret turned her head to him and said, He don't put his arm around me, see?

Put your arm around her.

Tony put his arm around her.

Then after a few more minutes she turned to Grampa. He's only touching the seat, see?

Grampa took hold of Tony's hand and laid it on Margaret's shoulder.

Again, one night, Grampa was waiting for him with Margaret. Okay—he was breaking into English now and then by this time—Okay, I'm going to sleep on the couch.

Tony had never slept in bed with her. He was afraid of Grampa because he knew he could never bring himself to raise a hand to him, and he knew that Grampa could knock him around; but it was not the physical harm, it was the sin he had been committing over and over again of trying to con the old man, whose opinion of him was falling every day, until one day, he foresaw, Grampa would pack up and take the trunk back to Calabria and good-bye. Grampa was no longer astounded by New York, and he still owned his house in Italy, and Tony visualized that house, ready at all times for occupancy, and he was afraid.

He went into the bedroom with Margaret. She sniveled on the pillow beside him. It was still light outside, the early blue of a spring evening. Tony listened for a sound of Grampa through the closed door, but nothing came through. He reached and found her hip and slid up her nightgown. She was soft, too soft, but she was holding her breath. He stretched his neck and rested his mouth on her shoulder. She was breathing at the top of her chest, near her throat, not daring to lay her hand on him, her face upthrust as though praying. He smoothed her hip, waiting for his tension, and nothing was happening to him until— until she began to weep, not withdrawing herself but pressed against him, weeping. His hatred mounted on the disappointment, tattletale sound she was sending into the other room, and suddenly he felt himself hardening and he got to his knees before her, pushed her onto her back and saw her face in the dim light from the window, her eyes shut and spinning out gray teardrops. She opened her eyes then and looked terrified, as though she wanted to call it off and beg his pardon, and he covered her with a baring of his teeth, digging his face into the mattress as though rocks were falling on him from the sky.

"Tony?"

He sat up in the darkness, listening.

"Hey, Tony."

Somebody was half whispering, half calling from outside the cable hole. Tony waited, uncomprehending. Margaret's teardrops were still in his eyes, Grampa was sitting out in the living room. Suddenly he placed the voice. Baldu.

He crawled out onto the catwalk. His helper was dimly lit by a yellow bulb yards away. "Looey?"

Baldu, startled, jerked around and hurried back to him on the catwalk, emergency in his eyes. "Charley Mudd's lookin' for you."

"Wha' for?"

"I don't know. He's lookin' high and low. You better come."

This was rare. Charley never bothered him once he had given the assignment for the shift. Tony hurried down the circular iron stairway, imagining some invasion of brass, a swarm of braid and overcoated men from the master's office. Last summer they had suddenly halted work to ask for volunteers to burn an opening in the bow of a cruiser that had been towed in from the Pacific; her forward compartments had been sealed against the water that a torpedo had

poured into her, trapping nine sailors inside. Tony had refused to face those floating corpses or the bloody water that
would surely come rushing out.

In the morning he had seen the blood on the sheets, and
Grampa was gone.

On B Deck, scratching his back under his mackinaw and
black sweater, Charley Mudd, alarmingly wide awake and
alert, was talking to a Protestant with an overcoat on and
no hat, a blond engineer he looked like, from some office.
Charley reached out to Tony when he came up and held
on to him, and even before Charley began to speak Tony
knew there was no way out, because the Protestant was
looking at Tony with a certain relief in his eyes.

"Here he is. Look, Tony, they got some kind of accident
on the North River, some destroyer. So grab a gang and
take gas and sledges and see what you can do, will you?"

"Wha' kinda accident, Charley?"

"I don't know. The rails for the depth charges got bent.
It ain't much, but they gotta go by four to meet a convoy.
This man'll take you to the truck. Step on it, get a gang."

"How do I heat iron? Must be zero outside."

"They got a convoy waiting on the river. Do your best,
that's all. Take a sledge and plenty of gas. Go ahead."

Tony saw that Charley was performing for the engineer
and he could not spoil his relationship. He found Hindu,
sent Baldu for his lunch from under the sailor's bunk, and,
cursing the navy, Margaret, winter, and his life, emerged
onto the main deck and felt the whip of a wind made of
ice. Followed by Hindu, who struggled with a cylinder of
acetylene gas held up at the rear end by Baldu, Tony
stamped down the gangplank to the open pickup truck at
its foot. A sailor was behind the wheel, racing the engine to

keep the heater going hot. He sent Hindu and Baldu back for two more cylinders just in case and extra tips for the burner and one more sledge and a crowbar and sat inside the cab, holding his hands, which were not yet cold, under the heater's blast.

"What happened?" he asked the sailor.

"Don't ask me, I'm only driving. I'm stationed right here in the Yard."

Forever covering his tracks, Tony asked how long the driver had been waiting, but it had been only fifteen minutes, so Charley could not have been looking for him too long. Hindu got in beside Tony, who ordered Looey Baldu onto the open back, and they drove along the donkey-engine tracks, through the dark streets, and finally out the gate into Brooklyn.

Baldu huddled with his back against the cab, feeling the wind coming through his knitted skating cap and his skin hardening. He could not bear to sit on the icy truck bed, and his knees were cramping as he sat on his heels. But the pride he felt was enough to break the cold, the realization that now at last he was suffering, striking his blow at Mussolini's throat, sharing the freezing cold of the Murmansk run, where our ships were pushing supplies to the Russians through swarms of submarines. He had driven a meat truck until the war broke out. His marriage, which had happened to fall the day after Pearl Harbor was attacked, continued to ache like a mortal sin even though he kept reminding himself that it had been planned before he knew America would enter the war, and yet it had saved him for a while from the draft, and a punctured eardrum had, on his examination, put him out of action altogether.

He had gone into the Yard at a slight cut in pay if figured

on hourly rates, but with a twelve-hour shift and overtime, he was ahead. This bothered him, but much less than the atmosphere of confusion in the Yard, for when he really thought back over the five months he had been here, he could count on one hand the shifts during which he had exerted himself. Everything was start and stop, go and wait, until he found himself wishing he could dare go to the yard-master and tell him that something was terribly wrong. The endless standing around and, worse yet, his having to cover up Tony's naps had turned his working time into a continuous frustration that seemed to be doing something strange to his mind. He had never had so much time to do nothing, and the shifts seemed endless and finally illicit when he, along with the others, had always to watch out for supervisors coming by. It was a lot different than rushing from store to store unloading meat and barely finishing the schedule by the end of the day.

It had never seemed possible to him that he would be thinking so much about sex. He respected and almost worshiped his wife, Hilda, and yet now that she was in Florida with her mother for two weeks, he was strangely running into one stimulation after another. Suddenly Mrs. Curry next door, knowing when he ate breakfast, was taking out her garbage pail at six in the morning with an overcoat on and nothing underneath, and even on very cold mornings stood bent over with the coat open for minutes at a time at the end of the driveway, facing his kitchen window; and every day, every single day now, when he left for work she just happened to be coming out the front door, until he was beginning to wonder if . . . But that was impossible; a fine married woman like her was most likely unaware of what she was doing, especially with her husband in the army, fighting Fascism. Blowing on his heavy woolen gloves, he was held by the vision of her bending over and thrust it furiously out of his mind, only to fall still, again remembering a dream he had had in which he was coming into his own bedroom and there on the bed lay his cousin Lucy, all naked, and suddenly he fell on her, tripped on the rug, and woke up. Why should Lucy have gone to bed in his room?

But now Brooklyn Bridge was unwinding from the tailgate of the truck, and how beautiful it was, how fine to be speeding along like this on a mission for the country, and everybody, even Tony, springing to action for the sake of the war effort. Baldu had to take off his cap and rub the circulation back into his scalp, and finally, feeling shivers trembling in his chest, he looked around and discovered a tarpaulin folded in a corner and covered himself. He sat under it in the darkness, blowing on his gloves.

Tony ate three spinach sandwiches out of his box, swallowing them a half at a time, like wet green cookies. Hindu had fallen silent, signaled by Tony's edgy look. The fitter was combative, turtled into his shoulders. As they crossed Chambers Street, the tall office and bank buildings they saw were dark, the people who worked in them at home, warm and smart and snug. Anybody out tonight was either a cop or a jerk; the defroster could not keep up with the cold, and the windshield was glazed over except for a few inches down near the air exhaust. Every curse Tony knew was welling up into his mouth. On deck tonight! And probably no place to hide either, on a ship whose captain and crew were aboard. *Margaret!* Her name, hated, infuriating, her sneaky face, her tattletale mouth, swirled through the air in front of him, the mouth of his undoing. For she had made

Grampa so suspicious of him that he still refused to open the trunk until he had evidence Margaret was pregnant, and even when she got big and bigger and could barely waddle from one corner of the small living room to the other, he refused, until the baby was actually born. Grampa had not earned his reputation for nothing—stupid men did not get rich in Calabria, or men who felt themselves above revenge.

As the last days approached and the three-room apartment was prepared for the baby, the old man started acting funny, coming over after dinner ostensibly to sit and talk to Margaret but really to see, as the three of them well knew, that Tony stayed at home. Nights, for a month or so now, he had followed Tony from bar to bar, knocking glasses out of his hand and, in Ox's, sweeping a dozen bottles to the floor behind the bar to teach Ox never again to serve his grandson, until Tony had to sneak into places where he had never hung before. But even so the old man's reputation had preceded him, until Tony was a pariah in every saloon between Fourteenth Street and Houston. He gave up at last, deciding to go with the hurricane instead of fighting it, and returned from the piers night after night now, to sit in silence while his wife swelled. With about eight or nine days to go, Grampa, one night, failed to show up. The next night he was missing too, and the next.

One night Tony stopped by to see if some new disaster had budded, like the old man's falling ill and dying before he could hand over the money, but Grampa was well enough. It was only his normally hard-faced, suspicious glare that was gone. Now he merely stole glances at Tony and even seemed to have softened toward him, like a man in remorse. Sensing some kind of victory, Tony felt the return of his original filial warmth, for the old man seemed to be huddling against the approach of some kind of holiness, Tony believed, a supernatural and hallowed hour when not only was his first great-grandchild to be born but his life's accomplishment would be handed down and the first shadow of his own death seen. The new atmosphere drew Tony back night after night, and now when he would rise to leave, the old man would lay a hand on Tony's arm as though his strength was in the process of passing from him to a difficult but proud descendant. Even Mama and Papa joined in the silence and deep propriety of these partings.

The pickup truck was turning on the riverfront under the West Side Highway; the sailor bent low to see out of the hand-sized clear space at the bottom of the windshield. Now he slowed and rolled down his window to look at the number on a pier they were passing and quickly shut it again. The cab was instantly refrigerated, a plunge in the temperature that made Hindu groan "Mamma mia" and pull his earflaps even lower. The night of the birth had been like this, in January too, and he had tried to take a walk around the hospital block to waste some time and could only get to the corner for the freezing cold. When he returned and walked back into the lobby, Mama was running to him and gripping him like a little wrestler, gulping out the double news. It was twins, two boys, both healthy and big; no wonder she had looked so enormous, that poor girl. Tony swam out of the hospital not touching the floor, stroked through the icy wind down Seventh Avenue, and floated up the stairs and found Grampa, and with one look he knew, he knew then, he already knew, for the old man's head seemed to be rolling on a broken neck, so frightened was he, so despondent. But Tony held his hand out for the key anyway and kept asking for it until Grampa threw himself on his knees and grasped him around the legs, hawking and coughing and groaning for forgiveness.

The trunk lid opened, Tony saw the brown paper bundle tied with rope, a package the size of half a mattress and deep as the trunk itself. The rope flew off, the brown paper crackled like splintering wood, and he saw the tied packets —Italian lire, of course, the bills covered with wings, paintings of Mussolini, airplanes, and zeros, fives, tens, colorful and tumbling under his searching hands. He knew, he already knew, he had known since the day he was born, but he ran back into the living room and asked. It had been an honest mistake. In Calabria, ask anybody there, you could buy or could have bought, once, once you could have bought, that is, a few years ago, until this thing happened with money all over the world, even here in America, ask Roosevelt why he is talking about closing the banks. There is some kind of sickness in the money and why should Italy be an exception, a poor country once you leave Rome. Hold on to it, maybe it will go up again. I myself did not know until two weeks ago I went to the bank to change it, ask your mother. I took the whole bundle to the National City in good faith, with joy in my heart, realizing that all your sins were the sins of youth, the exuberance of the young man who grows into a blessing for his parents and grandparents, making all his ancestors famous with his courage and manliness. It comes to seventeen hundred and thirty-nine dollars. In dollars that is what it comes to.

I used to make three hundred driving a truck from Toronto to New York, four days' work, Grampa. Seventeen hundred—you know what seventeen hundred is? Seventeen hundred is like if I bought one good suit and a Buick and I wouldn't have what to buy gas, that's seventeen hundred. Seventeen hundred is like if I buy a grocery store I be out on my ass the first bad week. Seventeen hundred is not like you got a right to come to a man and say go tie that girl around your neck and jump in the river you gonna come up rich. That's not nowhere near that kinda money, and twins you gave me in the bargain. *I got two twins, Grampa!*

The red blood washed down off his vision as the truck turned left and into the pier, past the lone lightbulb and the night watchman under it listlessly waving a hand and returning to his stove in the shack. Midway down the length of the pier shed, one big door was open, and the sailor coasted the truck up to it and braked to a halt, the springs squeaking in the cold as the nose dipped.

Tony followed Hindu out and walked past him to the gangplank, which extended into the pier from the destroyer's deck, and walked up, glancing right and left at the full length of the ship. Warm lights burned in her midship compartments, and as he stepped onto the steel deck he concluded that they might be stupid enough to be in the navy but not that stupid—they were all snuggled away inside and nobody was standing watch on deck. But now he saw his mistake; a sailor with a rifle at his shoulder, knitted blue cap pulled down over his ears and a face shield covering his mouth and chin, the high collar of a storm coat standing up behind his head, was pacing back and forth from rail to rail, on guard.

Tony walked toward him, but the sailor, who looked straight at him on his starboard turn, continued across the deck toward port as though in an automatic trance. Tony waited for the sailor to turn again and come toward him and then stood directly in his path until the sailor bumped into his zipper and leaped in fright.

"I'm from the Yard. Where's the duty officer?"

The sailor's rifle started tilting off his shoulder, and Tony reached out and pushed it back.

"Is it about me?"

"Hah?"

The sailor lowered his woolen mask. His face was young, and wan, with staring pop eyes. "I'm supposed to go off sea duty. I get seasick. This ship is terrible, I can't hold any food. But now they're telling me I can't get off until we come back again. Are you connected with—"

"I'm from the Navy Yard. There was an accident, right?"

The sailor glanced at Hindu, standing a little behind Tony, and then at both their costumes and seemed ashamed and worried as he turned away, telling them to wait a minute, and disappeared through a door.

"Wanna look at the rails?" Hindu joked, with a carefully shaped mockery of their order, shifting from one foot to the other and leaning down from his height to Tony's ear.

"Fuck the rails. You can't do nuttn in this weather. They crazy? Feel that wind. Chrissake, it'll go right up your asshole an' put ice on your throat. But keep your mouth shut, I talk to this monkey. What a fuckin' nerve!"

Looey Baldu appeared out of the darkness of the pier, carrying the two sledges. "Where do you want these, Tony?"

"Up your ass, Looey. Put 'em back on the truck."

Baldu, astounded, stood there.

"You want a taxi? Move!"

Baldu, uncomprehending, turned and stomped down the gangplank with the sledges.

The door into which the sailor had vanished opened, spilling the temptation of warm yellow light across the deck to Tony's feet, and a tall man emerged, ducking, and buttoning up his long overcoat. The chief petty officer, most likely, or maybe even one of the senior lieutenants, although his gangling walk, like a college boy's, and his pants whipping high on his ankles lowered the estimate to ensign. Approaching, he put up his high collar and pulled down his cap and bent over to greet Tony.

"Oh, fine. I'm very much obliged. I'll show you where it is."

"Wait, wait, just a minute, mister."

The officer came back the two steps he had taken toward the fantail, an expression of polite curiosity on his pink face. A new gust sent his hand to his visor, and he tilted his head toward New Jersey, from where the wind was pounding at them across the black river.

"You know the temperature on this here deck?"

"What? Oh. I haven't been out for a while. It has gotten very cold. Yes."

Hindu had stepped back a deferential foot or so, instinctively according Tony the air of rank that a cleared space gives, and now Baldu returned from the truck and halted beside Hindu.

"Could I ask you a little favor?" Tony said, his fists clenched inside his slit pockets, shoulders hunched, eyes squinting against the wind. "Would you please go inside and tell the captain what kinda temperature you got out here?"

"I'm the captain. Stillwater."

"You the captain." Tony stalled while all his previous estimates whirled around in his head. He glanced down at the deck, momentarily helpless. He had never addressed a commanding officer before; the closest he ever came in the Yard was a severe passing nod to one or two in a corridor from time to time. The fact that this one had come out on deck to talk to him must mean that the repair was vital, and Tony found himself losing the normal truculence in his voice.

"Could I give yiz some advice, Captain?"

"Certainly. What is it?"

"We can't do nuttn in this here weather. You don't want a botch job, do ya? Whyn't you take her into the Yard, we give you a brand-new pair rails, and yiz'll be shipshape for duty."

The captain half laughed in surprise at the misunderstanding. "Oh, we couldn't do that. We're joining a convoy at four. Four this morning. I can't delay a convoy."

The easy absoluteness shot fear into Tony's belly. He glanced past the captain's face, groping for a new attack, but the captain was talking again.

"Come, I'll show it to you. Give me that light, Farrow."

The sick watch handed him the flashlight, and the captain loped off toward the fantail. Tony followed behind. He was trapped. The next time he saw Charley Mudd . . .

The flashlight beam shot out and illuminated the two parallel steel rails, extending several feet out over the water from the deck. Two feet in from the end of the portside rail there was a bend.

"Jesus! What happened?"

"We were out there"—the captain flipped up the light toward the river beyond the slip—"and a British ship got a little too close trying to line himself up."

"Them fuckin' British!" Tony exploded, throwing his voice out toward the river where the Englishman must be. Caught by surprise, the captain laughed, but Tony pulled his hands out of his slit pockets and made a pleading gesture, and his face looked serious. "Why don't somebody tell them to stop fuckin' around or get out of the war!"

The captain, unaccustomed to the type, watched Tony with great expectation and amusement.

"I mean it! They the only ones brings cockroaches into the Navy Yard!"

"Cockroaches? How do—"

"Ax anybody! We get French, Norways, Brazils, but you don't see no cockroaches on them ships. Only the British brings cockroaches."

The captain shook his head with commiseration, tightening his smile until it disappeared. "Some of their ships have been at sea a long, long time, you know."

Tony felt a small nudge of hope in his heart. "Uh-huh," he muttered, frowning with solicitude for the English. Some unforeseen understanding with the captain seemed to loom; the man was taking him so seriously, bothering to explain why there were cockroaches, allowing himself to be diverted even for ten seconds from the problem of the rail, and, more promising than anything else, he seemed to be deferring to Tony's opinion about the possibility of working at all tonight. And better yet, he was even going into it further.

"Some of those English ships have been fighting steadily

ten and twelve months down around the Indian Ocean. A ship will get awfully bad that long at sea without an overhaul. Don't you think?"

Tony put gravity into his face, an awful deliberation, and then spoke generously. "Oh yeah, sure. I was only sayin'. Which I don't blame them, but you can't sit down on their ships."

Another officer and two more sailors had come out on deck and were watching from a distance as Tony talked to the captain, and he slowly realized that they must all have been waiting hours for him and were now wondering what his opinion was going to be.

With a nod toward the bent rail, the captain asked, "What do you think? Can you straighten it?"

Tony turned to look out at the damaged rail, but his eyes were not seeing clearly. The pleasure and pride of his familiarity with the captain, his sheer irreplaceability on this deck, were shattering his viewpoint. Striving to knit his wits together, he asked the captain if he could have the flashlight for a minute.

"Oh, certainly," the captain said, handing it to him.

Leaning a little over the edge of the deck, he shone the beam onto the bend of the rail. That pimping, motherfuckin' Charley Mudd! Look at the chunks of ice in that water—fall in there it's good-bye forever. In the skyscrapers at his back, men tripled their money every wartime day, butchers were cleaning up with meat so scarce, anybody with a truck in good shape could name his price, and here he stood, God's original patsy, Joe Jerk, without a penny to his name that he hadn't grubbed out by the hour with his two hands.

More than a minute had gone by, but he refused to give

up until an idea came to him, and he kept the light shining on the bend as though studying how to repair it. There had to be a way out. It was the same old shit—the right idea at the right moment had never come to him because he was a dumb bastard and there was no way around it and never would be.

"What do you think?"

What he thought? He thought that Charley Mudd should be strung up by his balls. Turning back to the captain now, he was confronted with the man's face, close to his in order to hear better in the wind. Could it be getting even colder?

"Lemme show you supm, Captain. Which I'm tryin' my best to help you out, but this here thing is a son of a bitch. Excuse me. Look."

He pointed out at the bend in the rail. "I gotta hit that rail—you understand?"

"Yes?"

"But where I'm gonna stand? It sticks out over the water. You need skyhooks for this. Which is not even the whole story. I gotta get that steel good and hot. With this here wind you got blowin' here, I don't even know if I can make it hot enough."

"Hmm."

"You understand me? I'm not trying to crap out on ya, but that's the facts."

He watched the captain, who was blinking at the bend, his brows kinked. He was like a kid, innocent. Out in the dark, river foghorns barked, testifying to the weather. Tony saw the sag of disappointment in the captain's face, the sadness coming into it. What the hell was the matter with him? He had a perfect excuse not to have to go to sea and maybe get himself sunk. The German subs were all over the coast of Jersey, waiting for these convoys, and here the man had a perfect chance to lay down in a hotel for a couple of days. Tony saw that the young man needed precise help, his feet placed on the road out.

"Captain, listen to me. Please. Lemme give you piece of advice."

Expressionless, the captain turned to Tony.

"I sympathize wichoo. But what's the crime if you call in that you can't move tonight? That's not your fault."

"I have a position in the convoy. I'm due."

"I know that, Captain, but lemme explain to you. Cut outa here right now, make for the Yard; we puts up a staging and slap in a new rail by tomorrow noon, maybe even by ten o'clock. And you're set."

"No, no, that's too late. Now see here"—the captain pointed a leather-gloved finger toward the bend—"you needn't true it up exactly. If you could just straighten it enough to let the cans roll off, that would be enough."

"Listen, Captain, I would do anything I could do for you, but . . ." An unbelievable blast of iced wind squeezed Tony's cheeks. The captain steadied himself, tilting his head toward the river again, gripping his visor with one hand and holding his collar tight with the other. Tony had heard him gasp at the new depth of cold. What was the matter with these people? The navy had a million destroyers—why the hell did they need this one, only this one and on this particular night? "I'm right, ain't I? They can't hold it against you, can they? If you're unfit for duty you're unfit for duty, right? Who's gonna blame you, which another ship rammed you in the dark? You were in a position, weren't you? It was his fault, not yours!"

The captain glanced at him, and in that glance Tony saw the man's disappointment, his judgment of him. He could not help reaching out defensively and touching the captain's arm. "Listen a minute. Please. Looka me, my situation. I know my regulations, Captain; nobody can blame me either. I'm not supposed to work unsafe conditions. I coulda took one look here and called the Yard and I'd be back there by now belowdecks someplace, because if you can't do it safe you not supposed to. The only way I can swing this, if I could swing it, is I tie myself up in a rope and hang over the side to hit that rail. Nobody would kick one minute if I said I can't do such a thing. You understand me?"

The captain, his eyes tearing in the wind, his face squeezing tight against the blast of air, waited for his point.

"What I mean, I mean that . . ." What did he mean? Standing a few inches from the captain's boyish face, he saw for the first time that there was no blame there. No blame and no command either. The man was simply at a loss, in need. And he saw that there was no question of any official blame for the captain either. Suddenly it was as clear and cold as the air freezing them where they stood—that they were both on a par, they were free.

"I'd be very much obliged if you could do it. I see how tough it is, but I'd be very much obliged if you could."

Tony discovered his glove at his mouth and he was blowing into it to spread heat on his cheeks. The captain had become a small point in his vision. For the first time in his life he had a kind of space around him in which to move freely, the first time, it seemed, that it was entirely up to him, with no punishment if he said no, nor even a reward if he said yes. Gain and loss had suddenly collapsed, and what was left standing was a favor asked that would profit nobody. The captain was looking at him, waiting for his answer. He felt shame, not for having hesitated to try, but for a sense of his nakedness. And as he spoke he felt afraid that in fact the repair would turn out to be impossible and he would end by packing up his tools and, unmanned, retreating back to the Yard.

"Man to man, Captain, can I ask you supm?"

"What is it?"

"Which I'm only mentionin' "—he was finding his truculent tone, and it was slowly turning ordinary again with this recollection coming on—"because plenty of times they run to me, 'Tony, quick, the ship's gotta go tonight,' and I bust my balls. And I come back next day and the ship is sittin' there, and even two weeks more it's still sittin', you understand me?"

"The minute you finish I'll be moving out into the river, don't you worry about that."

"What about coffee?" Tony asked, striving to give this madness some air of a transaction.

"Much as you like. I'll tell the men to make some fresh. Just tell the watch whenever you want it." The captain put out his hand. "Thanks very much."

Tony could barely bring his hand forward. He felt the clasping hand around his own. "I need some rope."

"Right."

He wanted to say something, something to equal the captain's speech of thanks. But it was impossible to admit that anything had changed in him. He said, "I don't guarantee nuttn," and the familiar surliness in his tone reassured him.

The captain nodded and went off into the midship section, followed by the other officer and the two sailors who had been looking on. He would be telling them . . . what? That he had conned the fitter?

Hindu and Looey Baldu were coming toward him. What had he agreed to!

"What's the score?" Hindu grinned, waiting for the delicious details of how Tony had outwitted the shithead captain.

"We straighten it out." Tony started past Hindu, who grabbed his arm.

"We straighten what out?"

"I said we straighten it out." He saw the disbelief in Hindu's eyes, the canny air of total refusal, and he felt anger charging into his veins. "Ax a man for a wood saw and a hammer and if they got a wreckin' bar."

"How the fuck you gonna straighten—"

"Don't break my balls, Hindu. Do what I tell you or get your ass off the ship!" He was amazed at his fury. What the hell was he getting so mad about? He heard Baldu's voice behind him, calling, "I'll get it!" and went to the gangplank and down to the pier, no longer understanding anything except the grave feeling that had found him and was holding on to him, like the feeling of insult, the sense that he could quickly find himself fighting somebody, the looseness of violence. Hindu had better not try to make him look like a jerk.

It took minutes for him to see again within the pier, where he walked about in the emptiness, shining the flashlight at random and finding only the bare, corrugated walls. Baldu came hurrying down the hollow-booming gangplank and over to him, carrying the tools. Another idiot. Son of a bitch, what did these guys do with themselves, jerk off instead of learning something, which at least he had done from job to job, not that it meant anything.

The flashlight found a stack of loading trays piled high against the pier wall. Tony climbed up the ten feet to the top tray. "What's this for?" Baldu asked, reaching up to receive it as Tony tipped it over the edge of the stack. He came down without answering and gestured for the wrecking bar. Baldu handed him the saw, blade first, and Tony slapped it away and reached over and picked up the hammer and wrecking bar and set about prying up the boards until the two five-by-five runners underneath were free. "Grab one," he said, and proceeded up the gangplank onto the deck.

He measured the distance between the two rails and sawed the runners to fit. It must be near eleven, maybe later, and the cold would be getting worse and worse. He cut two lengths of rope and ordered Baldu to tie the end of one around his chest, tied the other around himself, and then undid Baldu's crazy knot and made a tight one; he lashed both ropes to a frame at the root of the depth-charge rails, leaving enough slack for him and Baldu to creep out onto the rails. He took one end of a wood runner, Baldu took the other, and they laid themselves prone on the rails, then moved together, with the runner held between them, across the open water. He told Baldu to rest his end inside the L of his rail and to hold it from jarring loose and falling into the water, and he wedged his own end against his rail just behind where the bend began. He told Baldu to inch backward onto the deck, and Hindu to hand Baldu one of the sledges. But the sledges were still on the truck. He told them both to go down to the truck and bring the sledges, bring two tanks of gas, bring the burning torch and tips, and don't get wounded.

Baldu ran. Hindu walked, purposely. Tony sat on his heels, studying the rails. The sick watch paced up and down behind him in a dream. That fuckin' Charley Mudd, up to the ceiling by his balls.

"Hey, seasick," he said over his shoulder as the watch approached. "See if you can get me a tarp, huh?"

"Tarp?"

"Tarpaulin, tarpaulin. And step on it."

Christ, one was dumber than the other, nobody knew nuttn, everybody's fulla shit with his mouth open. What was the captain saying now, what was he doing? Had he been conned, really? Except, what could the captain get out of it except the risk of his life with all those subs off Jersey? If he had been conned, fuck it, show the bastard. Show him what?

Suddenly, staring at nothing, he no longer knew why he was doing this, if he had ever known. And somebody might fall into the water in the bargain once they started hitting with the sledge.

"Coffee?"

He turned and looked up. The captain was handing him a steaming cup and had two more in his other hand.

"Thanks."

Now Baldu and Hindu were clanking the gas cylinders onto the deck behind them. Tony drank his coffee, inhaling the good steam. The captain gave the two cups to the others.

"Whyn't you get off your feet, Captain? Go ahead, git warmed up."

The captain nodded and went off.

Tony put down his cup. The watch arrived, carrying a folded tarpaulin whose grommets were threaded with quarter-inch rope. Tony told him to put it down on the deck. He let Baldu drink coffee for a minute more, then told him to creep out on his rail and steady the wood runner while Tony hit its other end with the sledge to wedge it in tight between the two rails. Sliding the sledge ahead of him on his rail, he crept out over the water. At his left, Baldu, tied again, crept out wide-eyed. Tony saw that he was afraid of the water below.

Baldu inched along until he reached the runner and held it in the angle of the L tightly with both hands. Tony stood up carefully on his rail, bent down and picked up the sledge, then edged farther out on the rail to position for a swing. The water, in the light held by Hindu, was black and littered with floating paper. Tony carefully swung the sledge and hit the runner, and again, and again, and it was tight between the two rails. He told Baldu to back up, and they got the second runner and inched it out with them and wedged it snugly next to the first. Now there would be something to stand on between the two cantilevered rails, although it remained to be seen whether a man could bang the bent rail hard enough with so narrow a perch under him.

He unfolded the tarpaulin and handed one corner to Baldu, took the opposite corner himself, and both inched out over the rails again and tied the tarpaulin on the two runners so that it hung to the windward of the bend and might keep the air blast from cooling the steel. It might now. He backed halfway to the deck and told Hindu to hand

him the torch and to grab a sledge and stand on the little
bridge he had made and get ready to hit the steel.

"Not me, baby."

"You, you."

"What's the matter with the admiral here?" Hindu
asked, indicating Baldu.

"I wanchoo."

"Not me, baby. I don't like heights."

Tony backed off the rail and stood facing Hindu on the
deck.

"Don't fuck around, Tony. Nobody's payin' me to get
out there. I can't even swim good."

He saw the certain knowledge of regulations in Hindu's
mocking eyes. His own brows were lifted, his classic
narrow-eyed, showdown look was on his face, and never
before would he have let a man sneer at him like that without taking up the challenge, but now, strange as it was to
him, he felt only contempt for Hindu, who had it in him
to hit the beam much harder than the smaller Baldu could
and was refusing. It was a long, long time since he had
known the feeling of being let down by anyone; as long as
it was since he had expected anything of anyone. He turned
away from Hindu and beckoned to Baldu, and in the moment it took for Baldu to come to him, Tony felt sharply
the queerness of his pushing on with this job, which, as
Hindu's attitude proved, was fit for suckers and, besides, was
most probably impossible to accomplish with the wind cooling the steel as fast as it was heated. He bent over and
picked up the slender torch.

"You ever work a torch?"

"Well, not exactly, but . . ."

Tony turned to Hindu, his hand extended. "Gimme the sparker." From his jacket pocket Hindu took a spring-driven sparker and handed it to Tony, who took it and, noting the minute grin on Hindu's mouth, said, "Fuck you."

"In spades," Hindu said.

Tony squeezed the sparker as he opened the two valves on the torch. The flame appeared and popped out in the wind. He shielded it with his body and sparked again, and the flame held steady. He took Baldu's hand and put the torch into it. "Now follow me and I show you what to do."

Eagerly Baldu nodded, his big black eyes feverish with service. "Right, okay."

Unnerved by Baldu's alacrity, Tony said, "Do everything slow. Don't move unless you look." And he went to the bent rail and slid the sledge out carefully before him, slowly stretched prone on the rail and inched out over the water. He came to the two runners, from which the tarpaulin hung snapping in the wind, then drew up his legs and sat, and beckoned to Baldu to follow him out.

Baldu, with the torch in his left hand, the wind-bent flame pointed down, laid himself out on the rail and inched toward Tony. But with each thrust forward the torch flame swung up close to his face. "Let the torch hang, Baldu, take slack," Tony called.

Baldu halted, drew in a foot of tubing, and let the torch dangle below him. Now he inched ahead again, and as he neared, Tony held out a hand and pressed it against Baldu's head. "Stop."

Baldu stopped.

"Get the torch in your hand."

Baldu drew up the torch and held it. Tony pointed his

finger at the bend. "Point the fire here." Baldu turned the
torch, whose flame broke apart against the steel. Tony
moved Baldu's hand away from the steel an inch or two and
now trained it in a circular motion, then let go, and Baldu
continued moving the flame. "That's good."

It must be half past eleven, maybe later. Tony watched
the steel. The paint was blackening, little blisters coming
up. Not bad. He raised the tarpaulin to shield the flame
better. A light-yellow glow was starting to show on the
steel. Not bad. Gusts were nudging his shoulders. He saw
the tears dropping out of Baldu's eyes, and the flame was
moving off the rail. He slipped off a glove, reached over,
and pressed Baldu's eyelids, clearing the tears out, and the
flame returned to its right position. He saw that the watch
was pacing up and down again across the deck behind
Hindu, who was standing with the flashlight, grinning.

The yellow glow was deepening. Not bad. An orange hue
was beginning to show in the steel. He took Baldu's hand
and moved it in wider circles to expand the heated area. He
slipped his glove off again and pressed the tears out of Baldu's eyes, then the other glove, and held his hands near the
flame to warm them.

The steel was reddening. Stuffing the gloves into his slit
pockets, he drew up one foot and set it on the rail, leaned
over to the wooden bridge he had built and brought the
other foot under him and slowly stood erect. He bent slowly
and took the sledge off the rail and came erect again. He
spread his legs, one foot resting on the wood runners, the
other on the rail, and, shifting in quarter-inch movements,
positioned himself to strike. He raised the hammer and
swung, not too hard, to see what it did to his stability, and
the rail shuddered but his foot remained steady on it. He

brought up the sledge, higher this time, and slammed it down and under against the steel, one eye on the bridge, which might jar loose and send him into the water, but it was still wedged between the rails, resting on the flange of the L. Baldu was wrapping his free arm around the rail, and now he had his ankles locked around it too.

Tony raised the sledge and slammed down. The steel rang, and he heard Baldu grunt with the shock coming into his body. He raised the sledge and put his weight into it, and the steel rang and Baldu coughed as though hit in the chest. Tony felt the wind reaching down his back under his collar and icing his sweat. Pneumonia, son of a bitch. He slammed down and across at the rail and let the sledge rest next to his foot. The bend had straightened a little, maybe half an inch or an inch. His arms were pounding with blood, his thighs ached in the awkward, frightened position. He glanced back at Hindu on the deck.

"Not me, baby."

He felt all alone. Baldu didn't count, being some kind of a screwball, stupid anyway, he went around believing something about everything and meanwhile everybody was laughing at him, a clown who didn't even know it, you couldn't count on Baldu for anything, except he was all right, lying out there and scared as he was.

He was catching his breath, coughing up the residue of tobacco in the top of his chest. He glanced down and a little behind his shoe at the steel. It was deeply red. He pounded the steel rail, all alone—and rested again. It had straightened maybe another half inch. His breath was coming harder, and his back had tightened against the impossible perch, the tension of distributing his weight partly behind the hammer and partly down into his feet, which he dared not move. He was all alone over the water, the beam of the flashlight dying in the black air around him.

He rested a third time, spitting out his phlegm. The son of a bitch was going to straighten out. If he could keep up the hammering, it would. He dared not let Baldu hammer. Baldu would surely end in the water—him with his two left feet, couldn't do nuttn right. Except he wasn't bad with the torch, and the steel against his clothes must be passing the cold into his body. He glanced down at Baldu and saw again the fear in his face with the water looking up at him from below.

He raised the hammer again. Weakness was spreading along his upper arms. He was having to suck in consciously and hold his breath with each blow. Charley Mudd seemed a million miles away. He could barely recall what Dora looked like. If he did decide to go through with the date, he would only fall asleep in her room. It didn't matter. He let the sledge rest next to his foot. Now it was becoming a question of being able to lift it at all. Hindu, to whom he had given a dozen phone numbers, was far away.

Tony licked his lips, and his tongue seemed to touch iron. His hand on the sledge handle seemed carved forever in a circular grip. The wind in his nose shot numbness into his head and throat. He lifted the sledge and felt a jerky buckling in his right knee and stiffened it quickly. This fuckin' iron, this stubborn, idiot iron, lay there bent, refusing his demand. Go back on deck, he thought, and lay down flat for a minute. But with the steel hot now, he would only have to heat it all up again, since he could not pass Baldu, who would also have to back onto the deck; and once having stopped, his muscles would stiffen and make it harder to start again. He swung the hammer, furiously now, throwing his full weight behind it and to hell with his feet—if he fell off, the rope would hold him, and they had plenty of guys to fish him out.

The rail was straightening, although it would still have a little crook in it; but as long as he could spread it far enough from the other one to let the cans pass through and into the sea, some fuckin' German was going to get it from this rail, bammo, and he could see the plates of the sub opening to the sea and the captain watching the water for a sign of oil coming up. He rested the sledge again. He felt he was about to weep, to cry like a baby against his weakness, but he was a son of a bitch if he would call it off and creep back onto the deck and have Hindu looking down at him, both of them knowing that the whole thing had been useless.

He felt all alone; what was Hindu to him? Another guy to trade girls with and buddy with in the bars, knowing all the time that when the time came he'd give you the shaft if it was good for him, like every man Tony had ever known in his life, and every woman, even Mama, the way she told on him to Grampa, which if she hadn't he would never have had to marry Margaret in the first place. He smashed the sledge down against the steel, recklessly, letting his trunk turn freely and to hell with falling in.

"That looks good enough!"

For a moment, the sledge raised halfway to his shoulder, he could not make out where the voice was coming from, like in a dream, a voice from the air.

"I'm sure that's good enough, fella!"

Carefully turning his upper body, he looked toward the deck. The captain and two other men and the watch were facing him.

"I think you've done it. Come back, huh?"

He tried to speak, but his throat caught. Baldu, prone, looked up at him, and Tony nodded, and Baldu closed the valves and the flame popped out. Baldu inched backward along the rail. A sailor reached out from the edge of the deck and grabbed the back of his jacket, holding on to him until he slid safely onto the deck and then helping him to stand.

Out on the rail, the sledge hanging from his hand unfelt, Tony stood motionless, trying to educate his knees to bend so that he could get down on the rail and inch back onto the deck. His head was on crooked, nothing in his body was working right. Slowly now, he realized that he must not lie down anyway, or he would have to slide his body over the part of the rail that was probably still hot enough to scorch him. Experimentally he forced one foot half an inch along the rail but swayed, the forgotten weight of the sledge unbalancing him toward his right side. He looked down at his grasping hand and ordered it to open. The sledge slipped straight down and splashed, disappearing under the black water. The captain and the crewmen and Baldu stood helplessly in a tight group, watching the small man perched with slightly spread arms on the outthrust spine of steel, the rope looping from around his chest to the framework on the deck where it was lashed. Tony looked down at his feet and sidled, inch after inch, toward the deck. Joyfully he felt the grip of a hand on his arm now and let his tension flow out as he stepped off the rail and onto the deck. His knee buckled as he came down on it, and he was caught and stood straight. The captain was turning away. Two sailors held him under the arms and walked him for a few steps like a drunk, but the motion eased him and he freed himself. A few yards ahead, the captain slowed and, glancing back, made a small inviting gesture toward the midships section, and pushed by the wind went through a doorway.

He and Baldu and Hindu drank the coffee and ate the buns. Tony saw the serious smiles of respect in the sailors' faces, and he saw the easy charm with which Hindu traded jokes with them, and he saw the captain, uncapped now, the blond hair and the way he looked at him with love in his eyes, saying hardly anything but personally filling Tony's cup and standing by and listening to Hindu with no attention but merely politeness. Then Tony stood up, his lips warm again and the ice gone out of his sweat, and they all said good night. As Tony went through the door onto the deck, the captain touched him on the shoulder with his hand.

When Hindu and Baldu had loaded the gas tanks onto the truck with the sledges, Tony indicated for Baldu to get into the cab, and the helper climbed in beside the sailor, who was racing the engine. Tony got in and pulled the door shut and through the corners of his eyes saw Hindu standing out there, unsmiling, his brows raised, insulted. "It's only midnight, baby," Tony said, hardly glancing at Hindu. "We got four more hours. Git on the back."

Hindu stood there for twenty seconds, long enough to register his narrow-eyed affront, then climbed onto the open back of the truck.

Outside the pier the sailor braked for a moment, glancing right and left for traffic, and as he turned downtown Tony at the side window saw sailors coming down the gangplank of the destroyer. They were already casting off. The truck sped through the cold and empty streets toward Chambers and Brooklyn Bridge, leaving it all behind. In half an hour the destroyer would be back in its position alongside the cargo ships lined up in the river. The captain would be where he belonged. Stillwater. Captain Stillwater. He knew him. Right now it felt like the captain was the only man in the world he knew.

In the Yard, Tony made the driver take them up to the drydock where the cruiser lay on which they had been working. He went aboard with Baldu, without waiting for Hindu to get off the back, and found Charley Mudd and woke him up, cursing the job he had given him and refusing to listen to Charley's thanks and explanations, and without waiting for permission made his way through the ship to the engine room. Overhead somebody was still welding with the arc too far from the steel, and he raised his collar against the sparks and climbed up to the dark catwalk and found the cable passage and crawled in, spreading himself out on the steel deck. His body felt knotted, rheumatic. His smell was powerful. He went over the solutions he had found for the job and felt good about having thought of taking the runners off the loading tray. That was a damn good idea. And Baldu was all right. He visualized the kink that remained in the rail and regretted it, wishing it had been possible to make it perfectly straight, but it would work. Now the face of the captain emerged behind his closed eyes, the face uncapped as it had been when they were standing around having coffee, the blond hair lit, the collar still raised, and the look in his eyes when he had poured Tony's coffee, his closeness and his fine inability to speak. That lit face hung alone in an endless darkness.